B.E.A.R.
llionaire

TERRY BOLRYDER

TERRY BOLRYDER

CHAPTER
ONE

JANNA SAT WITH HER FRIENDS at the best table the gorgeous mountain lodge had to offer. It was on the upper floor overlooking the main hall and provided a great view of both the front door and the majestic, white-tipped mountains rising up around the isolated lodge.

In the small tourist town of Bearstone Park, there wasn't a lot to do other than mingle with (or avoid) tourists. But the Bearstone lodge had become a fun place for the women to go once a week to catch up on their lives.

When Janna had first moved and found herself alone in a new place with no way to leave and nowhere to go, she'd found kindred spirits in Leslie and Kylie, and the three had been fast friends ever since.

"Oh my gosh," Leslie murmured, setting down her mug and letting her jaw hang open as she stared at the front door. Janna turned to see what her friend was looking at.

"Wow," Kylie said. "And doesn't the one in the middle look familiar?"

"They *all* look vaguely familiar," Janna said, narrowing her eyes on the three tall—no—enormous men entering the room and silencing it with their beauty.

The first was the most intimidating.

Dark hair curling around his face and collar in rough waves, a sharp face with dark eyes that were a clear, sparkling deep blue, even from a distance.

Janna felt her heart skip a beat when the man looked up into her eyes. A slow grin spread over his face. She blushed and pulled her chair back a bit, making herself less visible as she looked at the other men.

"Oh, the one on the end," Kylie said, pointing at a tall man with golden-blond hair, ice-blue eyes, and a muscular, toned build. He wore a ski jacket and had his hands in his pockets, looking over the place like he was already bored.

"I recognize him. He was just in the X Games last year, wasn't he? Didn't he take gold in the half-pipe?"

"I think you're right," Leslie said. "Ryan... something?"

"Hart," Kylie said, biting her lip and squirming a little in her chair.

Janna grinned at her friend's overt attraction to the man below. Kylie was such a shy, bookish type but always tended to go for the athletes. Janna didn't watch the X Games, so she couldn't say she recognized the tall man, but she had to admit his only rival in beauty were the two other men standing with him.

Janna did, however, recognize the third man, who was standing between the other two.

His hair was a medium brown, slightly waved, with golden highlights strewn throughout, and he had tanned skin and hazel eyes. He was handsome, no doubt about it. But he also had a face that almost anyone in the world knew.

"Holy crap, that's..."

"I know... Riley Hart."

Kylie shook her head. "Do you think they're all related?"

Janna didn't answer. Her gaze had wandered, as if pulled by a magnet, back to the man who was leading the trio forward. Did she recognize him from anywhere? She must. What else would make it so hard to peel her eyes away? Her whole body felt melted into liquid want the longer she looked at him.

He and his brothers towered over everyone in the room, at around 6'7", and he was clearly the leader, with his dark looks and sharp eyes. And when they reached the front of the room and talked to the front desk, she swallowed, trying to tear her gaze from his perfect, taut ass.

"I recognize *him*, too," Leslie said, nudging Janna.

"What?"

"The one you're slobbering over. That's Ryder Hart. The tech mogul."

Janna's throat tensed and her heart stuttered. "I've heard of him. I didn't know he looked like that."

"Honestly, Janna, it's like you've been living in a box."

Janna shrugged, knowing they were right. Ever since she'd moved here and been so utterly disappointed, she'd not been very interested in men in general, preferring to simply work and keep her mind off the thought of any kind of future that involved males. And she had Leslie and Kylie to keep things interesting and to talk to if she got lonely.

Judging by the looks on her friends' faces, however, neither of them suffered from any of the same hang-ups. "You want to go talk to them, don't you?" Janna asked.

Leslie nodded. "Let's go."

Kylie fidgeted. "Are you sure? I mean, they could talk to anyone in the room."

Leslie grinned, eyes sparkling, and tossed her soft, dark curls back over her shoulder. "That's the thing, though. We're women, and men like that will probably prefer our company to that of the hunters and hikers down there."

"Oh," Kylie said quietly, blushing as her eyes targeted in on Ryan's ass again.

Janna set her mug down and looked at it drearily. When did she lose the ability to be excited when a beautiful man appeared? Maybe after she followed the last beautiful man who showed interest and it landed her here.

Her friends tittered about their plans to go approach while she sulked over her mug, but then she felt eyes on her. It was unmistakable. She was being watched. And just knowing it made her heat up inside, made her body forget the promises her mind was trying to keep to herself.

Just one night with a man like that…

No, she couldn't think that way. She had a job now, a life, and friends. She didn't need to be wrapped around a man's finger. And Ryder Hart, with that devilish blue gaze, could definitely throw her life out of whack again.

RYDER HART WAITED FOR THE front desk clerk with a rising sense of irritation. He couldn't wait to make his move on the gorgeous brunette on the upper balcony. Her pretty dark skin and warm, sparkling brown eyes had caught his eyes the moment he walked in out of the cold.

Warmth at a time when he desperately needed it. He didn't know exactly what it was that drew him to her, but he knew he wanted to get up there quickly and find out more about her.

The only trouble seemed to be she didn't seem to eager to meet him, withdrawing from view when he had smiled at her. But he didn't become a billionaire by not being able to close a deal and overcome objections.

What Ryder wanted, Ryder got.

And what Ryder wanted right now was to get his damn key and head up with his brothers to meet the luscious ladies and potential mates on the second floor.

"Which one do you like?" Riley asked, propping his sunglasses atop his head. With his tanned skin, killer smile, and pretty-boy features, Riley was braver with the women than either he or Ryan. Part of it might have to do with the fact that as the star of several breakout romantic films, there didn't seem to be a woman in America or elsewhere that didn't recognize him. Thus the sunglasses, even in the dead of winter.

"None," Ryan said, folding his arms and leaning lazily against the counter. "I'm planning on you two being the ones to find mates while I kick back on the slopes."

"Come on, bro, I promise there's more to life than snowboarding," Riley said, teasing.

Ryan shrugged. "If there is, I haven't found it."

"What about that little blonde checking you out up there?" Riley asked, nodding.

Ryan looked up to where Riley gestured and then shook his head, though Ryder thought he was more affected than he was trying to appear. "Pass. Not interested."

"Ah, why not?" Riley asked. "Can I have her, then?"

Ryan sucked in a breath and let it out slowly. "See if I care."

"What about you?" Riley asked Ryder.

Ryder kept his face carefully neutral. He didn't want competition from his brothers on this. "The one in the middle."

"Which one? Not the angry-looking one."

Ryder frowned. "She doesn't look angry."

"Um, bro, yeah, she totally does," Riley said, throwing his arm around Ryder's shoulder. "Not good. I'd tell you to go for the one with the curls, but I thinks she's going to warm *my* bed tonight."

Ryder shook his head. "Don't mess with the locals, Riley. We have a job here, remember? It won't be good if you go getting on people's bad sides in a small town."

"Shit, I didn't think of that," Riley said, scratching his head. "Now what am I going to do?"

"Maybe keep it in your pants for once?" Ryan snapped.

"Yeah, because that's what bears are known for," Riley scoffed.

But then the clerk handed Ryder his key and his brothers' banter faded into the distance. All he could see were warm, sparkling brown eyes watching him once again. And this time, he saw the quick bite of her lip that told him exactly what he needed to know.

She *was* affected by him; she just didn't want to be. He started toward the stairs, not one to wait when he knew what he wanted.

"Wait, bro, hold up!" Riley jogged after him and Ryan followed. "Don't you want to get our stuff to the room and unpack?"

"You can do it," Ryder said. "I think I've found my mate."

"Already?" Riley asked, eyes wide. "You're kidding."

"Who?" Ryan asked.

"None of your business," Ryder retorted, scowling. "Now if you'll excuse me…"

Riley scoffed. "Yeah, right. We're coming."

"We're totally coming," Ryan agreed.

Ryder heard and ignored them. He was a bear on a mission.

JANNA SIGHED WHEN THE HANDSOME man disappeared from view. Her friends were now trying to figure out what the men were doing in town and whether they should let them settle in before approaching.

Maybe it was time for her to call it a night and head out before the snow got worse.

"Guys?" she asked, interrupting them and pulling their attention her way. "I'm tired. I think I'm going to head home."

Leslie sighed in disappointment. "Ah, you can't go. We'll stop the boy talk. It's girls' night after all. We haven't even heard about Scott's weekly shenanigans."

Kylie nodded, also interested.

Janna's stomach felt sour at the thought. She'd had fun regaling her friends with stories of her stupid ex and his exploits to get her back, but as he'd been getting more aggressive, it had become more unpleasant to talk about. And she didn't want to admit it was honestly getting to the point that it was making her nervous.

"He hasn't done anything of note this week," Janna said quietly.

"Darn," Leslie said, frowning. "He's just so lame. It's karmic justice to watch him failing all over the place with you."

Janna nodded. When Scott had cheated, she'd felt the ground beneath her crack in half. Now he couldn't have half that effect on her. He could still, however, make the ground shake a little. And she wished more than anything that he would just let her move on.

But when his woman on the side moved, he'd suddenly become interested in Janna again, which just affirmed what Janna already knew. That his relationship with her had been all about fulfilling needs and nothing else.

Still, Janna knew she was a smart, independent woman who had made a life for herself in this town even after tragedy, and that sustained her whenever he had the gall to come around.

Not that she'd complain if he stopped.

"You ladies mind if we join you?" A smooth, deep voice cut in. "We're new in town."

Leslie was the bravest and the first to look up. Janna knew it would be the men from below. The voice was so heart-meltingly sexy it could only match up with one of those gorgeous faces.

"Sure, join us," Leslie said, and Janna groaned inwardly.

She tried to ignore the men, but she felt a chair pulled up right next to her, felt the heat of a large, male body beside her. Not touching, but close enough. She gritted her teeth and looked up into intent, deep blue eyes that made her breath catch in her throat.

Ryder Hart was even handsomer up close. Handsome wasn't a strong enough word. With sharp features that could cut ice, long lashes, and unruly dark hair, he was movie-star gorgeous. Sort of like his movie star brother. But there was a keen intelligence in those dark blue eyes, and as he raked her from head to toe with his gaze, Janna got the feeling this was a man who was much more than his appearance.

Then he had the gall to reach out and touch her hair. And she had the gall to let him.

She drew in a short breath and felt warmth spread over her body as the rest of the table went quiet and watched them. He drew her hair behind her ears and leaned in closer, eyes still locked on hers, and then gazed down at her lips.

What was going on? It was like being caught in a spell. Maybe it was just because she hadn't been with anyone in so long. Janna licked her lips and saw his eyes heat, and in the moment, she felt so beautiful, so utterly desirable because of that look, that she almost melted on the spot.

But then Scott's face flashed in her mind and she sucked in a breath and pulled back, swatting away his hand. The spell was broken, and she heard awkward laughter from the others at the table. The man stood up abruptly, anger in his eyes. He folded his arms and appraised her as if he didn't understand how or why she'd rejected him.

Janna ignored him and drank her coffee, avoiding Leslie's wide-open eyes and Kylie's dropped jaw. Of course they wouldn't understand how she'd turned down such a good-looking, powerful man. But Janna had experience with good-looking, powerful men. And the faster and smoother the approach, the less she generally trusted them.

Janna pinned the man with a look (when she was calm enough to not appear openly aroused by him) and pushed his empty chair further away with one foot. "I don't know where you're from, but here it's not polite to touch strangers before even introducing yourself," she said.

His gaze on her was intense, and she inwardly cursed as she found herself being the one to break eye contact. Looking at him too long did something to her, something she didn't like. Something that made her feel out of control, and Janna hated nothing so much as being out of control.

RYDER'S HEART POUNDED, AND HE told himself to calm down. Being rejected by the woman he was more and more sure was his mate had hurt him deep, but he knew she was a human. She didn't know what he did, that it was something you could know in an instant. She affected him to his core just when he was touching her hair.

Ryder wasn't often physical with women. He was always working, and not in touch with his bear lately. But one look at the woman's tall, curvy body had the animal in him begging to break out and claim her this instant.

But this would take time. He could tell by his mate's wary face that she didn't trust him, didn't trust most people maybe, and wouldn't be the type to get easily swept off her feet by someone like him.

He sat on the chair she pushed to him. Even though the alpha in him resisted the idea of letting her control the conversation, he decided that strategically, the best move was to let her think she was running things.

"Fine," he said, "I'll introduce myself, then. I'm Ryder Hart, and these are my brothers, Riley and Ryan." He gestured to them as they sat. "And we're here to run the lodge until my father's will can be worked out."

"Wait, was your father Royce?" the curly-haired woman asked. "Grumpy, huge Royce?"

"One and the same," Riley said, flashing her a wink that had her blushing. If only the woman Ryder had his eye on seemed half as open to advances.

But maybe that's part of what he liked about her, in addition to the stirrings inside him that said his bear wanted her. She didn't look like she was desperate or dependent. She stood on her own two feet, waiting for the right partner. Now Ryder would just have to prove it was him.

"I'm Leslie," the curly-haired one said. "And this is Kylie." She motioned to the smaller blonde. "And Janna," she said, gesturing to the woman Ryder had nearly kissed.

Janna. A beautiful name, Ryder thought as he more carefully studied the woman he'd set his sights on. She had a heart-shaped face with smooth, warm-brown skin, beautiful red lips, and thick, unruly hair that a man could wrap his hands in. And a body made to be loved by a bear like him.

Soft, large, warm. His mouth watered at the thought of holding her against him. His whole body responded to the thought, and he scooted his chair back slightly in shock.

Riley sent him a knowing look, and Ryder resisted the urge to smack him. But alphas didn't smack. Not in front of potential mates.

The others started to talk, but the woman, Janna, simply wouldn't open up or join in. Ryder watched her as Riley flirted shamelessly with the other two. She seemed totally detached, in another world, as she studied her cup like there was something interesting at the bottom.

Was he really so undesirable as a mate that she couldn't even look at him?

She stood suddenly, planting her hands on the table. "Excuse me, but I've got to head back," she said quietly, looking at her friends with a silent message he couldn't read.

Leslie looked regretful, and Kylie seemed to be reluctant to pull her eyes from Ryan's face, but both Leslie and Kylie stood in solidarity. "Sorry, guys," Leslie said. "Looks like we gotta head out." She gestured out the window. "Snow is getting bad, and we need to get back to town."

"When can we see you again?" the little blonde, Kylie, asked.

"Whenever you want," Riley said, winking at her and making her blush from head to toe. "We're going to be staying here for a while."

"Maybe not that long," Ryan grumped.

The blonde flinched.

Ryder felt bad for her. She was setting her eyes on the wrong male. Ryan might be a bear, but he was a bear more interested in staying in the wild than being domesticated.

And as for Riley, in whom Leslie seemed to be interested, well, Ryder doubted Riley would ever be happy with less than a full harem.

But for him, he'd always known just one would be perfect, if it were the right one. Someone to raise a family with, to run in bear form with, to play with cubs with. And he could see all that in Janna's clear brown eyes. She stood and pushed past him, not even acknowledging him as he stood.

The three women left, only two of them promising to come back. He'd been thoroughly rejected.

But he wasn't offended.

Ryder never shied away from a challenge.

CHAPTER
TWO

JANNA SHUFFLED THE PAPERS IN front of her absent-mindedly and then put them in a folder. She couldn't get the man from the night before out of her mind.

Blue eyes, like a sapphire night, like a lake under the stars, twinkled in her mind, making it hard to keep her mind on her work or even focus on what she was supposed to be doing today. The end of the year was coming and tax season would hit soon, and she needed to get her other work up to date before all hell broke loose. As the only accountant and tax professional in a tiny tourist town, Janna was the main person people depended on to keep their businesses straight.

A small bell jingling over the door alerted her to someone entering, and she looked up to see Scott.

She noticed with some small satisfaction that his fine, blond hair was thinning and the lines on his forehead were deepening. She didn't think it was fair for such an awful person to be so handsome, and she thought it was about right that he was losing his looks now.

He didn't seem to think he was, however. She could tell from the cocky glow in his gray eyes that in his mind, he was still the hottest thing in town and any woman should simply feel blessed to be in his presence. Someone should tell him that as of last night, that was no longer true.

As of last night, he was at least three ranks lower on the hotness totem pole.

Her mouth watered as she shoved the papers haphazardly into a file. Each of the men from last night was an amazing specimen of the best mankind had to offer. The fact that they were all together was startling. The fact that they were also brothers was mind-blowing.

The fact that she could think about them now, with Scott's presence both threatening and obnoxious in the distance, was something she'd rather *not* think about.

"Seems like you're doing all right for yourself here," Scott said sardonically, walking forward into the store in a relaxed posture, hands in his too-tight Chino pockets, wearing a leather jacket over his worn, pink designer polo. Scott was the picture of average success and above-average looks, with his smooth skin and boyish good looks that were only slightly marred by his wrinkles.

But Janna knew beneath the good looks was a personality that was less than ideal. Less than normal. Less than desirable. But that didn't stop her heart from aching just slightly at what she'd thought she wanted. Security and a home with him. Even now, as he eyed her with what he must feel was a charming look, a part of her wanted nothing to have happened between them. For her to never have found out what he was doing behind her back. So they could go back to what they were. When she was happy.

At least she'd thought she was happy.

Maybe, in all reality, all she'd been was comfortable.

Certainly, looking into Ryder Hart's sapphire eyes, she had seen the promise of everything except comfortable. Life with him, even at its best, would never be anything like it was with Scott.

Not that she knew him enough to know much about him. But something about his intimidating presence, the sense that he took no crap from anyone and he took care of his business, made her think life with him would never be easy, but it also would never be full of the cowardly crap Scott had dished out.

"You okay?" Scott asked, taking another unwelcome step into the room toward the front counter. "You seem a little out of it."

Her heart skipped a beat and she kept her eyes on the folder she'd just closed. She never knew what to say to Scott. A part of her felt that if she talked to him at all, it'd be letting him win in his game of trying to pretend nothing had happened. That he could just start over pursuing her and she'd fall at his feet once again.

Maybe that would have been true before. When she was new to this town and alone and younger and not sure she could stand on her own two feet. But now she was certain. She had friends in Leslie and Kylie and a life here with a successful and busy business, and she didn't need stupid Scott interfering.

But how to tell him that without actually talking to him? She really felt if she spoke to him, she'd start yelling and never stop.

"You're going to have to talk to me at some point, Janna," Scott said. "You can't just keep ignoring me. Not in a town this small."

She sighed. He should have thought of that before he cheated on her. Yes, they'd be trapped alone in this small town. He probably thought since she didn't have many options, she'd come back to him eventually, regardless of how he'd treated her. But that simply wasn't how things had worked out, thank heavens.

Sapphire-blue eyes winked in her mind again. Maybe she should be a little less standoffish. Maybe just so she didn't have to look at Scott.

But then, when she first met Scott, hadn't things been so much more exciting and promising? Maybe she was forgetting how it all went down. Maybe she was just trying to distract herself or hoping for rescue from an awkward situation. Whatever it was that had made her think Ryder Hart was an option, it also seemed to have called him out of thin air, because the bell over the door rang a second time as his large presence filled the room.

Maybe it was just the cold air that blew in at his bold entrance, maybe it was just the way his broad shoulders filled the room and the way his simple elegance bespoke wealth and power in a style Scott couldn't achieve with ten times the effort.

Janna told herself it was just the cold winter air causing her breath to catch in her chest, but an uncomfortable tightening in her legs as she met Ryder's eyes told her otherwise.

Gosh, she got turned on just by looking at him. Had she even fallen for Scott this instantly? She berated herself for being a silly woman and planted her hands on the counter to stay steady. She noted with some pleasure that Scott wasn't pleased at all by the disturbance the newer, larger man caused.

Ryder, for his part, cocked an eyebrow at Scott and pulled his lips into a frown that suggested the other man should just disappear. Scott quickly complied, flashing Janna a look that said this was far from over. She sighed and rested back on the standing stool behind the counter.

"Did you need help with something?" she asked Ryder, who was still just standing there, hands in the pockets of his expensive black ski jacket, dark hair tousled by the wind and snow. When she spoke, his eyes flashed and locked on hers. She bit her lip in response and then flushed when his eyes moved down to her mouth.

"If I did, would you help me?" he asked, a bit of a tease in his words— and something darker. Something that made her press her legs together in anticipation. "You weren't very friendly the other night."

She pressed her lips together and tried to look relaxed on her chair. She didn't often have billionaire tech investors in her shop, and when she did, they didn't have movie-star good looks. "Well, I guess it depends on the type of help you need." She nodded behind her. "But if you need accounting help, I'm probably your only option in this town."

He exhaled as if disappointed that their banter was gone and there was actual business talk in its place. "Fine. Business it is. I need your help with the books up at the lodge."

"Really? I thought the lodge had Barry?"

Barry had been the other accountant in town, but he worked exclusively for Ryder's father. She was sure he was paid well enough that it hadn't been an issue.

Ryder's handsome face tightened and an angry flush heightened the color on his high cheekbones. "We discovered some… issues. He was let go."

She swallowed. Had Barry been embezzling? She'd never liked the man, with his cranky, pinched look and the little smirk he gave her when they crossed each other on the road. But she'd just put it down to him not liking that they were competitors. "I'm sorry to hear that."

Ryder waved her concern away with one hand. Probably the amount of money that Barry had taken was a tiny amount compared to the fortune this billionaire possessed. She wondered why he was even back here at all. She couldn't remember ever seeing him around here before.

Gosh, she just wanted to hole up with him in a cabin for the winter and let him tell her everything about his life. By the hot, appraising look he gave her as she sized him up, she had the feeling the sentiment was somewhat mutual.

But why did she get the feeling that Ryder Hart had deeper secrets than anyone could fathom?

A chill went through her as the door opened and closed, and a little old lady named Ada came in to schedule a later time to work on some tax issues. She concluded the business quickly, trying not to feel Ryder's eyes on her with each breath, but by the time Ada had given her a quick hug and left, she was all too aware of the presence of the large man in front of her.

"So what can I help with?" she asked. She pushed a signup sheet toward him. "Want to work out a time to come in and go over your books with me?"

He slowly removed leather gloves, revealing smooth hands and long fingers. This was a man who had made his fortune with his mind, not his brawn, though from the muscles bulging through his winter clothing, it was clear there was plenty of that as well.

"I was actually hoping you could come up to the lodge with me. I think it'll take a good amount of time to go through what we need to go through. And I'd hoped to get to know you better while we were at it."

She blushed at the words "at it," thinking just what she would like them to imply. Oh no, she was doing it again. Getting romantic and dreamy-eyed and getting way too many ideas about where things could go. For the past year, she'd been the cool, cold accountant, and that had suited her fine. Everything by the numbers.

Nothing about Ryder Hart would be by the numbers.

She bit her lip as she tried to decide whether she'd give him his way.

"You know you'd be buying only my accounting services, right?" she said nervously. "Nothing more. I don't know if you're the type who thinks you can walk in and buy the local women, but I assure you, women here have their choice of partners same as anyone, and we don't need men coming in and assuming we're waiting here for someone to rescue us."

His lips pressed into a hard line and his expression grew colder as she finished. "Are you done?" he asked sharply. "I can assure you I have the highest of ethical expectations of myself as well as others. All I'd really ask of you is that you put whatever baggage is obviously bothering you behind you while we work together." A small grin tipped up the corners of his lips. "And if we should decide to take our relationship beyond the professional, it should only be because you find me as irresistible as I find you, Janna."

His grin deepened as he approached the counter and placed a finger under her chin. She gulped. So close. Those sapphire eyes seemed to go on and on. She pulled back, snapping her chin out of his grasp and taking deep breaths to try and undo the hold he had on her.

"Don't count on it," she grated out, folding her arms over her chest to hide her heightened breathing. "Don't count on it, *Ryder Hart*."

He raised an eyebrow as he stepped back. "Ah, so you know who I am? I couldn't tell from your lack of response at my earlier introduction." He took out his phone and checked it, tapping it a few times with a tense expression before placing it back in his pocket. "Well, then you should know what Ryder Hart wants, Ryder Hart gets. And when I set my mind on an acquisition, it's only a matter of time before it's mine."

Her heart beat hard at that. "I'm not something to be acquired," she spat out angrily. "And I can't work with you if you see it that way."

He shrugged and threw out a number. "That's what I'll pay you for coming up to the lodge. Should take only a few days, maybe a week, max. Think it over."

Her heart stammered. That was enough to get her out of the lousy mortgage on this place and happily settled in civilization. "Why would you pay me that?" she asked suspiciously. "There's no way I'm worth that."

He gave her a hard smile that didn't quite reach his eyes. "Then maybe you aren't giving yourself the correct valuation." He held out a hand. "Do we have a deal or not?"

She eyed him skeptically. She didn't know if she should really trust this mysterious man, but then again, if he did anything untoward, there were about a million journalists who would want to hear about it.

She bit her lip and thrust her hand into his. He caught it and jerked up the sleeve in a smooth movement to place a kiss on the top of her hand.

"Perfect," he said. "Looking forward to working with you. I have a few more errands in town. I'll pick you up in an hour, sound good?"

She blinked. She'd need to call in someone to schedule things and watch the store, but that shouldn't be too hard. Sherry from the grocery store had been looking for more hours. And it wouldn't take long to pack.

And a part of her just hadn't been on an adventure in so long that she couldn't wait another minute to get started on something with this powerful, mysterious man.

And unlike last time, at least if this man broke her heart, she wouldn't be left alone in the middle of nowhere. He was her ticket out of this life, and she intended to take it.

"Fine," she said, feeling like she was sealing her fate. "One hour."

He nodded and pulled up his hood to head back into the cold. She bit her lip and held back her sigh until he disappeared back into the storm.

CHAPTER
THREE

RYDER WAITED ANXIOUSLY IN HIS Range Rover. He could have taken the limo to town, but he preferred the sense of absolute control that came from being behind the wheel. Control that the storm kept trying to take from him. He made a note to find out exactly what the best method for being the safest on snow was. Ryder didn't like anything interfering with his ability to control things, especially when it came to safety.

Living and working in Silicon Valley ever since the tragedy years ago, he'd almost forgotten how bad weather could make driving. And now that he'd be driving his potential new mate home, he had to steel himself against the rush of nerves that came when he thought of the night he'd learned exactly how powerful a bit of frozen water could be.

But he hardened his heart against the sensation and turned down the music when he thought he heard the sound of a door opening and closing. He slid out of his seat and shut the car door behind him as he hurried up to her walk. Janna looked beautiful as usual, her dark curls swirling about her head, those sparkling eyes blinking away the snowflakes battling to get past her long lashes, those plush, red lips pursed against the wind as she struggled with her suitcase, which Ryder hefted easily away from her and over his shoulder as he wrapped an arm around her and guided her down the walk.

She gave him a grateful, though still a little dubious, look and came with him to the car. He got the door open and ushered her in, shut the door, and then hurried around to the back to put in her oversized suitcase. What a woman would need for a few days to a week that could take up such a huge amount of space he didn't know. He just knew he could barely believe he'd closed the deal and gotten her to come with him.

Now came the hard part.

A world of tech negotiations and million-dollar business deals still hadn't given him much experience with women. Sure, a few beautiful women here and there at parties or coming on to him after business meetings, but no one that had ever given him the instant, hungry attraction he'd had when he saw Janna.

When he saw her, he knew it was forever. If he could win her, that is.

But he still didn't forgive his father, he thought as he swung up into his seat and closed his door against a whoosh of air. When his father had demanded in his will that his sons come back and find mates in the tiny town where they'd grown up, he couldn't have known there'd be a beautiful, feisty woman like Janna waiting for him.

Even now, she was sitting with a backpack on her lap, back rod straight, red lips pursed stubbornly. This was a woman who wouldn't make things easy, and Ryder already liked that about her. Hell, maybe that's why he'd been drawn to her in the first place.

"Anywhere you need to stop before we head up into the mountains?" he asked.

"No," she said, pouting slightly.

"Not having second thoughts, are you?" he asked. He'd prefer if his future mate didn't feel he was being too pushy about this. He didn't want her looking back with any regrets. Then again, he had a feeling he couldn't give her a lot of time before claiming her. He'd seen the man in the store that had been here before him. The confusion and hurt in Janna's eyes. This was the bastard who'd put all that doubt there, and the bastard clearly wasn't done causing the damage he intended.

But Ryder intended to insure he didn't get the chance to finish what he'd started. The man wanted Janna, but Ryder would make sure he never got her. Even if she didn't choose him. He could sense the other man was the type who actually saw women as acquisitions, which is something Ryder found disgusting. Anything between him and Janna would have to be more of a merger.

He grinned at the thought of it and put the car into gear, enjoying the way Janna eyed the luxurious interior. He didn't need a lot of money or nice things himself, but he thought he wouldn't mind if Janna could benefit from some of the hard work he'd been doing.

But he hadn't done it for the money. He'd done it for the same reason he'd done many things. The control. The power. The pursuit. The rush. The competition.

And sure, seeing that jerk in Janna's store had fired that innate sense of competition within him, but Ryder had been set on Janna since the night he came to her table. Maybe he wasn't that experienced with women, but he could tell by the way she blushed, the way she tried to hide her squirm when he locked eyes with her, that she was affected too. Now he had her for a week. He just needed to woo her.

But how did one do that? He was grateful he'd have Riley, the gross playboy, to give him some tips. He could always toss out the distasteful ones. He was sure Riley, as a celebrity, had a different way of getting women and a different taste for them than he, Ryder, did.

"You okay?" she asked. "You're awfully quiet. Something you haven't really been with me."

Ryder cleared his throat. Damn, he had a habit of getting lost in his mind when he was nervous and trying not to be. But she was just so beautiful, and now that he'd gotten her to agree to come with him, his mind was racing on how to move forward without screwing it up. "Fine, just concentrating on the storm. These roads can be dangerous. I want you to feel safe with me."

She grinned. "That's sweet of you. But I've been up these roads many times in much less safe cars. We like to have girls' night at the lodge, remember?"

He growled. "I don't like the sound of that. What if you got hurt? We've had accidents on this road, you know. People were killed."

She sighed. "Not all of us have fancy cars, Mister Billionaire. And I'm not giving up my girls' nights for anything. It's all I have in this little town."

"Yeah, I can't imagine living here really," he replied. Even though he could. In a little cabin, just the two of them, until cubs came along. He wet his lips and focused on the road, as he was supposed to be doing. "So who was the guy that came in before me?"

He regretted it the minute it came out. But the jealous part of him, the part that didn't want to share any part of her with anyone else already, couldn't help wanting to know everything he could about his potential future rival. It was the business shark in him, maybe. Scope out the competition. Find out their weaknesses. Attack.

"Oh. Um. An ex."

His stomach twisted in an unpleasant way. He knew it was a little odd that he was falling this hard, this fast, but according to his father, this was how it had been between him and Ryder's mother. Ryder hated his father for being a player, but he had to admit he admired him for knowing what he wanted and going after it. It was the selfishness that came after that Ryder couldn't accept. Damn it, would he end up like that if he mated? No, it was monogamy for him all the way. Besides, with his work, he'd barely have time for anything else.

But he had a feeling after ignoring his bear for so long, he'd be taking some time off work when he found a mate. Or at least taking it a little easier.

Ryder focused on the road, which was still icy but better now that the snow was lessening. The wipers made a kind of unpleasant intrusion into the silence, reminding him he really should have something to say about now. But bears were solitary creatures, so even his animal couldn't help him with this one.

Bear shifters were rare and didn't reproduce as easily as wolves or other shifters did. That was probably part of why his father had pulled them all back here to find mates. Probably there were some women around with latent bear blood or women who were just hardy in general if they could live out here in the cold, isolated weather in the winter.

Women who could perhaps carry bear shifter cubs.

He stifled a growl as he tried to think of a way to ask about her ex that wasn't intrusive. But he couldn't, so he just stayed silent, unable to believe he could already feel so possessive of a woman he'd barely met.

"So what brings you to Bearstone Park?" she asked quietly. "Must be pretty different for a big tech mogul like yourself."

He sighed and clenched one hand around the wheel. "Actually, I grew up here. At least for while. Anyway, Dad's will brought us back."

He snuck a look at her and caught her biting her lip and eyeing him sideways. He snapped his gaze back to the road. Just the one second look at her, those lush lips bitten in just the way he'd like to bite them, had made his pulse increase.

Easy, Ryder.

"But if you didn't want to come back, I doubt there's anything in his will that could tempt you. I mean, you're one of the richest men in the world."

Ryder nodded. It was true but only because his dad had given them all something to start out with. He'd gone into investing and done very well for himself after business school. But it was more than that. His father had given him life in a world where life wasn't easy to give. He had a duty to reproduce, and his father would know more about it than most. And with so little family, bear shifters took family ties seriously. Especially without a mother around.

His heart throbbed at that and his chest tightened painfully, as if to shield the long-buried wound there.

"You're kind of a still-waters-run-deep kind of person, aren't you?" she asked.

He laughed at that, palming the wheel to take a careful turn and rubbing the ache from his chest, hoping she didn't notice. "I don't know. I can be quite loud and forceful when the time calls for it, or even when it doesn't. You can ask my brothers about that. I guess being home just sort of feels nostalgic."

"So your brothers will be there too?"

He opened his mouth to say yes, that they were also there looking for mates, but then jealousy ran through him. "They'll be around, yes. But you'll be working mainly with me." Damn, that sounded controlling. But best she get used to it now. If she became his mate, he'd be that much more possessive. Much as he loved them, his brothers were the last people he'd want spending much time alone with his potential future mate.

That was his bear talking. His bear had sized up the woman with her curves and her beautiful ass and made up its mind on the spot. Ryder would just have to follow because the same bear had driven him to success in the business world with its strength and tenacity, and he had no doubt its taste in women were awesome as well.

It didn't hurt that it made Ryder's mouth water to think about those luscious curves under his hands. He was a big, tall man, and he could easily handle those bountiful, lush breasts, that wide, plush ass. He gripped the wheel a little tighter and hoped she didn't notice the sudden tightness in his pants.

"So I'll be staying at the lodge?" she asked. "Fancy."

He swallowed, grateful for the change of subject. "Yes. Or one of the cabins, which are even nicer."

"Thanks," she said. "I've always wanted to stay there."

"Why haven't you?"

"Spendy," she replied.

He shook his head. "I'll have to talk to Mark about setting up a locals-only rate. It's not right that the lodge should be supported by a town that can't even afford to enjoy it."

"Well, we do enjoy meeting up there, but that's nice of you. I think a lot of people in town would take you up on it. But wouldn't you lose money?"

"That's not how I like to make money. Excluding people who are poor. And we aren't usually fully booked, even in tourist season. The lodge is just too big."

"Ah. Right," she said lightly, and he panicked, wondering if the conversation was boring her. The last thing he ever wanted her to feel in his presence was boredom.

"So tell me about this ex," he said as they rounded a turn that put the large lodge in sight in the distance. He almost caught his breath at the view. Large mountains covered in snow rising up on either side, white-laden pines swaying in a blurry haze. Beautiful white all around. "You didn't seem happy to see him." Well, it was out on the table now. Hopefully she wouldn't be mad at him for bringing it up.

She let out a sigh full of confusion and pain, and his throat tightened. His bear was almost too good at reading into any sound or vocalization, and he simultaneously regretted bringing up something painful but was grateful that if she needed to share something with him, she could.

"It's a long story. You want the long or the short version?"

"Whichever you want to tell me."

She laughed. "You're good with women, you know that? I wouldn't have guessed on first meeting you."

"I came on too strong, didn't I?"

She leaned on the window and eyed him playfully. He made an effort to keep his eyes on the road, though he knew the route by heart. "A little. I guess I haven't had anyone come on to me in a while."

"I find that hard to believe," he said a little too forcefully. "I mean, you're beautiful. I'm sure the men in this town are just fighting over you constantly."

"Hm, fighting? I don't know about that. I think most of them still probably see me as Scott's property. Lots of the folks here are old-fashioned, and it doesn't help that he owns the bank and a lot of their mortgages. Including mine."

"Not good," Ryder said. "He doesn't look like the type I'd want handling my mortgage."

"He's the only game in town," she said quietly.

"Not anymore."

"Right," she said with a sigh. "Anyway, we met online. I thought it was amazing that this handsome, successful guy could be so interested in me. And we met up a few times. I fell in love with the town when I visited. He convinced me to move out. I foolishly jumped at the chance to open my own business. But really, I think I felt he was my last chance. I'm shy, and I'd never really met anyone. No one who showed as much overt interest."

Ah, so that was why she'd been wary around him. She already jumped in it once with a guy who came on too strong, too fast. But this was different. Ryder was a bear, and his bear was instinctive, but never wrong. And he'd just have to prove that to her. While keeping this other jackass away, of course.

"Anyway, shortly after I moved here, selling everything I had to do so, Scott cheated. Well, I discovered him cheating. I guess he could have been cheating before that, but that's when I found him. I felt so stupid. I couldn't go back to my family, who'd done nothing but say 'I told you so,' and I had nothing left. So I settled." Heavy silence hung over them while she thought. "But anyway, I thought he was done. But a few months later, after his girl on the side left town, he was back. Thinking, I guess, the fat girl in town wouldn't have any other options."

He snorted. "Fat girl?"

She shook her head. "Look at me."

"I have been," he said, grinning. "Ever since I first laid eyes on you. You're beautiful, curvaceous. If you want to call it fat, fine. But I call it the kind of body that was made for a big man like me."

"Rude!" she said, but then she laughed, and he knew she was warming to him. Good. He'd just have to keep her warming to him.

"You're hot, babe. That's all there is to it. He tried to have his cake and eat it too, and now he realizes what he let get away. Men often do, you know. When they cheat."

"Do what?"

"Realize they gave up the best thing for them." He tried to keep the bitterness out of his tone. If his dad had truly felt this way about his mom, why had he treated her like that? Why had he strayed? He clenched his hand around the steering wheel and tried to force the thoughts from his mind. He had his father's journal to read through while he worked through the will, and maybe more answers would be forthcoming. In the meantime, he was angry.

"I'm sorry if I hit a sore spot," she said quietly.

"Well, let's just say the old man had a little bit of Scott in him," he replied, hating the sourness that came from admitting it. "Anyway, have you told this Scott guy that you're not interested?"

"I've been refusing to talk to him. If I try to tell him, if I give him a reason, he's the type that will just try to argue me out of it. If I ignore him, there's nothing he can do."

A prickle of unease went up Ryder's back. For what could have happened when he wasn't around. This didn't sound like a person who was simply interested. The fact that he'd been trying to keep contact when she'd been outright ignoring him made him something worse than simply an ex. It made him a stalker. And who knew what was on his mind. And who would inflict more pain and annoyance on a woman they'd already hurt badly?

"Why don't you call the cops?" he asked.

"He knows the cops," she said. "They'd probably just tell me he doesn't mean any harm and I should forgive him, besides. Anyway, I don't want to talk about Scott anymore. I'm fairly certain he couldn't reach me up here, and I'm going to savor that."

"And if he did, I'd toss him out on his ass. And then some," Ryder grumbled, fury moving through him as they pulled up the final drive to the lodge, rising huge in the distance.

"What?" she asked.

"Nothing," he snapped, not sure if she'd be okay with him showing his overprotective nature this early. But he wouldn't let anything happen to Janna, not while she was here with him. Not in general, even if she didn't choose him. She was clearly a good woman, and he'd free her from the presence of Scott in her life one way or another. If it was a ticket out of here she wanted, then the money he'd pay her for this week would be sufficient to grant that.

The thought made him a little queasy though. Janna leaving.

She's not yours yet, he told his bear. His bear turned up his nose with a huff as if to say he didn't believe him.

His bear was such a powerful animal that he often felt more separate to Ryder than a part of him. Yet without both sides of him, he wouldn't have been whole. Both separate and the same, him and his bear.

And his bear was excited to pull up at the lodge safely with Janna.

Game on.

CHAPTER
FOUR

JANNA WRAPPED HER ARMS AROUND herself as she stepped out of the car. Ryder had come around to hold her door, and she felt an ache of nostalgia at how it felt to have someone taking care of her. She hadn't been courted in what felt like forever.

But she knew guys like Ryder didn't go for women like her. They usually had young, slender models or Hollywood starlets on their arms. Sometimes both at once.

It wasn't that Janna didn't see herself as a smart, independent woman who'd seen hardship and proven herself by getting through it. It was just that after catching Scott in the arms of a skinny woman, just when she'd dared to believe a man could love her just as she was, the insecure teenager in her had come roaring to life, reminding her that guys never end up with the fat girl.

Stop it, she told herself inwardly. *That's past baggage, and Ryder deserves a fair shot.*

None of her usual alarm bells were going off with him. But maybe that was just that perfect smile, those deep blue eyes that sparkled like a night sky over the mountains in summer, or that tall, immensely muscled body that made her feel small and petite. Two things she really wasn't.

It's not that she didn't care. She worked out and ate all right for a busy professional. But she didn't have the time to devote all day to fitness or the metabolism to be naturally thin. And she'd been chubby since she was little and just kind of embraced it. Unlike her sister, Beth, whom her mom had always favored, no matter what she did, it didn't seem to result in her being skinny.

So she'd resorted to being the independent girl. The smart girl. The successful one. While Beth had ridden on her looks and married rich men. Three different times.

She sighed at the thought that she should probably call and check in on her family but told herself putting it off another week wouldn't matter.

"Something wrong?" Ryder asked, hefting her heavy suitcase like it weighed nothing and reaching for the backpack she was holding in front of her.

"No," she said quietly, looking up at the lodge, and the man in front of it, and trying not to be intimidated. Both the man and the building were rough, powerful, and strong. Hewn seemingly from the wilderness. Hard as rock. But she could tell from the quirk in Ryder's lips that there was also softness there. "Just thinking."

"I guess we have that in common," he said, slinging the backpack over his shoulder and extending an arm for her to take. Her hand barely wrapped around his bulging bicep and she swallowed as a wave of arousal made her almost woozy. What was up with the effect this man had on her?

"What in common?" she asked, feeling off kilter.

"Getting lost inside our heads. Common thing for intelligent people, you know. I find myself thinking a lot when I should maybe be participating in conversation instead. But it's just that—"

"The thoughts in your head interest you more?" she asked, sharing a grin with him as she finished his sentence. When she let her reservations go, it was nice to have met someone whom she seemed to click with immediately.

Now, if only she could get over her own insecurity and the fact that he was rich as Croesus while she was struggling to pay her mortgage due to the poor interest rate Scott had given her. She was an accountant, she knew better, but she'd been heartbroken and not all the way there mentally. All her issues were on high alert, distracting her from reading the fine print.

A mistake she made sure she never made with her clients. But then again, a theme of her life was she tended to treat other people better than she treated herself.

"So tell me more about you," he said, walking up to the lodge and then taking a little road off to the side.

She cocked her head curiously but followed him anyway. "Not much to tell. Moved from San Diego. Raised there with a normal family. Got a finance degree." She shrugged but felt her hackles rise slightly as they moved into the woods around the lodge. "Where are we going?"

"I thought maybe I'd set us up with something special," he said, walking toward a cabin a few yards away. "Keep you out of the main lodge where you might be bothered by the noise level."

"I don't remember it being loud before," she said.

"That was before Riley Hart was in residence," he said. "I'd rather you didn't have to be a part of the kind of parties he throws."

"Must be weird having a brother who's a movie star," she said. "And a heartthrob at that."

"Well, we haven't lived near each other in a long time. And I get enough press on my own. And then there's Ryan, with his Olympic career. I guess when you're high profile yourself, it's not as big a deal to have high-profile siblings."

"Hm," she said, not entirely convinced. Damn, she liked the look of his back as he pulled away from her to unlock the front door of a cabin. So wide, so tall. She guessed he'd have no trouble carrying her to the bedroom, if he wanted to. The thought made her blush and squirm, eager to get inside away from the cold and put her mind to unsexy thoughts, like unpacking and their work schedule together.

Together. Damn, that was a word that kicked off the heat in her again, and she wondered once more at her odd connection to Ryder Hart. She'd seen him in magazine articles once or twice and couldn't remember ever feeling anything but admiration. But the man in person? Pure liquid lust. Which wasn't usual for logical, rational Janna.

Ryder set down her things and then flipped on a light. Then he went about the cabin, which was more like a pricey, five-star suite, checking to make things were in order.

"Would you like me to get the fire going?" he asked.

A real fire. The smell, the feel. It was tempting. She bit her lip. Sitting in front of the fire with Ryder…

"Or would you like to get dinner?" he asked, picking up her things and taking them through a door off to the side. He disappeared for a moment and reappeared without the bags. "I was thinking we could get takeout from the lodge."

"I don't know," she said. "This all happened so quickly. I mean, you only gave me an hour to pack."

He shrugged, not looking at all abashed for having whirlwinded into her life and made everything complicated. "I had to move fast. Lover boy there didn't look very patient."

"My love life isn't your concern," she said patiently. *Yet.*

He frowned. "I told you, Janna. What I want, I get. And I want you. Yes, right now, I want your expertise with financial matters up at the lodge. Mainly to check me as I go over things to make sure I'm not screwing them up. I'm better with big picture than small details like bookkeeping. But aside from going to hire an accountant, my next job in town would have been to find out where you lived and go to meet you and somehow convince you to come back here with me and give me a chance."

"A chance?" She swallowed against the lump in her throat. As a financial analyst, she knew better than most that if it sounded too good to be true, it probably was.

"Yes, a chance. I like you. I liked you from the moment I saw you, and I think you like me."

"Maybe," she said, not meeting his eyes. If he looked into her own, he'd see the lust burning there. He'd think she was a woman that easily fell for a man, when the opposite was true.

He shed his jacket as the cabin warmed. She could hear the heater running. The room was well lit, with gorgeous leather furniture and rustic wood decor that was probably specially carved for the lodge and its adjoining buildings. For city people to feel like they were roughing it. It would have worked on her if Scott had brought her.

But apparently, she hadn't been good enough for that.

But with Ryder, she was.

He looked even broader and taller without the coat. His massive shoulders pushed against a blue cashmere sweater just slightly darker than his eyes. His biceps and forearms more than filled out the sleeves, and he'd pushed them up slightly, baring beautiful wrists and hands. Fine hands with long, strong fingers. Fingers he'd used to tilt her chin just that afternoon. Fingers that could do wicked things that made her wet just thinking of them.

He took a couple dangerous steps forward, and Janna felt her pulse speed up. Was Ryder Hart a player? She couldn't remember reading anything non-business about him. She bit her lip and tried to hide a shuddering breath as he looked down at her, nearly close enough to touch. He put a finger beneath her chin and lifted her gaze to his.

That's it, she thought. *He can see it. He knows.* Sure enough, she met his eyes and saw triumph lighting there in the sparkling blue. She squirmed slightly and his arms came around her, holding her up.

"This is so unprofessional," she said weakly, pressing against his chest, only to have the feel of his firm muscle make her feel even weaker.

"Mmm," he said, leaning forward to nip the top of her ear. "Sometimes unprofessional is more fun." His hand caressed her waist and moved toward her bottom, and she pulled away. He wrapped both arms around her instead and looked down.

Gosh, he was handsome. That jaw was cut from granite, just a hint of a cleft in his chin. Full, pouty lips with a sculpted cupid's bow. High, carved cheekbones.

He put a hand up to caress her hair and his thumb brushed the top of her cheek. "Tell me to stop, Janna, and I will."

She blinked, body rebelling against her mind. Her mind said this was dangerous. That she'd only gotten carried away once in her life and it had ended badly, so she should run from this. But her body kept saying how good it felt to be in Ryder's arms and how long it had been since she'd been with a man. Maybe if she just didn't have any expectations, maybe if she just assumed he'd leave at the end, maybe they could just have some fun together and that would be all. And it wouldn't have to hurt or disappoint her after.

She knew her place. Ryder was probably looking for a week of fun and then to forget.

But judging from the electric feel of his hands on her body, her hormones were up for whatever he wanted.

As long as he didn't stop touching her.

"What's wrong?" he asked, pulling away slightly, making her body ache with need at the loss of contact.

She shook her head and pulled away with great effort and slumped over the couch.

"I just… I barely know you. This makes no sense. I don't want you to think I'm the kind of woman who… well, makes rushed decisions."

"Would it matter if you were?" he asked, sitting next to her, making her feel small even when they were both seated. "Would it affect what happens between us? I want to get to know you, Janna. Just who you are."

"But why?" she asked. "You could have anyone in the world. How do I know you aren't just killing some time while working out your father's business. I'm sorry, but guys like you don't go for girls like me. Not without a catch."

"A catch?"

"Like Scott," she said nervously, pulling down her sweater.

Ryder's face hardened and he drew up to his full, intimidating height. "I'm nothing like him. He's an ass."

She laughed, slapping her knee. "It feels good to hear that, you know? But the thing was I didn't think he was an ass then."

"So you learned. But are you going to hold every man accountable to that? Why don't you let me show you something different?" He leaned forward and the air heated between them. "You know I'm different."

She licked her bottom lip and looked at his mouth. Those lips on hers... it would feel amazing. Surely she deserved a little fun after so long.

His gaze shifted to her mouth and he sucked in a ragged breath. The next moment, his lips were on hers. Sliding gently over until he found the perfect fit between them. Just warm, solid softness, light breaths, and a careful caress of his soft lips on hers. She sighed into it and opened without thinking, and his strong, deft tongue swiped inside, claiming, caressing, stroking, each movement making her a little hotter, a little weaker, a little achier in that place that kept responding to him against her better judgment.

He came forward, moving her back on the couch until he had her against the armrest. His hand wrapped around to cradle her head and tangle in her hair, and his other hand moved down her body, feeling each curve in his strong hand as if he were trying to memorize the feel of her. He drank in kisses, the feel of her soft curves, like a hungry man finding bounty, and she melted in his arms.

Ryder Hart was a kissing god.

She opened farther and met his tongue with hers, clashing, circling, moaning as he explored every sensitive spot within her mouth, making her think of a different kind of way he could be inside her, making her legs tighten and twist in anticipation and a tingling sensation settle between her thighs.

He seemed to sense it, and an excited growl rumbled from his chest as one hand moved to her breast. He caught her gasp of surprise as one deft finger flicked over her nipple, which was sticking out even in her bra. The sharp, pleasurable sensation had her arching back, and his hand covered her breast in a firm knead as he deepened the kiss even further.

She was past conscious thought. Past rational analysis. This was nothing by the numbers. This was fantasy, pleasure, joy all caught up in one moment, and she didn't want it to end. She no longer wanted to question it. Whatever the cost was, she'd pay for it later.

And even though she knew with a slight ache that's what had gotten her in trouble in the first place, she had no ability to say no to Ryder or this undeniable pleasure now.

He pulled back to massage both her breasts. He growled with satisfaction, and she could barely believe the lust burning in his eyes as he studied her expression. His thumbs moved over her sensitive nipples and she arched back with a low moan.

"You're beautiful, Janna," he murmured, pulling off her sweater with a smooth motion, revealing her in only a lacy lavender bra that contrasted her silky brown skin. "So amazingly beautiful. I could lick you all over."

She couldn't say anything, just arched to give him access to the back of her bra, which he undid easily, freeing her breasts.

"Oh hell yes," he said, cupping her soft flesh in both hands. She knew she was large there, but his huge hands cradled her perfectly. "You're so perfect, Janna. You bring out the animal in me."

She saw something feral flash in his eyes, but she didn't know how to describe it. And once he took one of her nipples in his able, hot mouth, she didn't want to. Pleasure shot through her and she clenched her legs together again, almost as if her body were trying to deny her what she wanted. His hand moved between her thighs, parting her legs and putting one of his between them, holding her legs open. He finished sucking her nipple and flicked his tongue over it. She cried out and arched back at the sudden sensation.

He was too much and not enough all at once. She ached for him in her most sensitive place and found herself rubbing wantonly against his hard thigh. Thankfully, he moved back, sliding up against her with delicious friction that eased the ache inside her, but only somewhat. She needed him inside her, now.

But he seemed intent on taking his time, moving his huge leg against her while his hands kneaded her sensitive breasts and his lips took hers again, his tongue delving deep, promising rhythmic ability in other activities. He left her mouth to press kisses to her cheek, her jaw, her neck, and then stroking along the sensitive inner shell of her ear with a deft motion that had her crying out as his thigh pressed once more into the apex of her pleasure.

She hit her release with him touching her everywhere, owning her body, and keeping the rhythmic contractions going again and again as he moved against her, setting all of her nerves on overload and making her cry out over and over for relief from the overwhelming pleasure. When she finally settled, she found him pulling his shirt over his head.

She flushed in relief. She needed him inside her. Now. She'd never moved this fast, but she knew if she didn't have this now, she'd always regret it. She could think about that later. Right now all she could think about was having the hard length of that thing bulging the front of his jeans buried inside her, warm and stimulating and stretching her as never before. Something like that, she'd never forget.

The clink of his buckle and zip of his jeans heated her fever and she pulled at her own pants helplessly. He pulled hers down easily, fingers grazing her soft thighs in wonder as he let out a groan of agony at how hot she was. He leaned down to place a kiss at the top of her damp panties, and she arched to let him. He pulled them off with a quick flick of his fingers and she was bared to him. But she felt beautiful, desirable. She no longer cared that he was a famous billionaire and she was just average. He was just a man about to take her as a woman, and every nerve in her body screamed for it to be so.

He was free of his pants a second later, and she gasped at the size of him as he sprang free from a pair of tight boxer briefs. Would he fit? He put on a condom. She squirmed in anticipation and he licked his lips and positioned himself over her. He felt her with his fingers and smiled as he licked her wetness off.

"So wet for me, sweetheart," he said.

She nodded. It was too late for embarrassment.

"I'll try not to hurt you," he said. "I know I'm large."

She swallowed, trying to stay relaxed as she felt his huge tip at her entrance. If she got him in, she was in for one hell of a ride. Just as she tensed, she felt his hand gently moving over her tummy to relax her, moving up to caress her breast as he placed a soft kiss at her jawline and then moved to take her mouth.

As his tongue thrust in, so did the rest of him, taking her channel in one swift movement that had her writhing in shock against the sudden, incredible fullness. She gasped against his mouth and he stroked a hand comfortingly over her skin, running along her side and cupping her bottom to hold her against him.

She took a few deep breaths and the fullness adjusted to something else. Incredible pleasure, once she could distinguish it from the panic of being so full. He was right against her G-spot, pressing it hard, lighting her up with sensation, and then he started to move.

She screamed and dug her hands in. She couldn't help it. The feel of his firm hardness moving inside her, going deep and thick against every sensitive millimeter of her pussy, made her feel like no one else ever had. When he was nearly out, and her body exhaled in relief, he pushed back in again, and she gasped and cried out as her body accommodated him. It was heaven; it was almost too much to take. And she could see from the determined, tense look in his eyes that he was equally overcome by the sensations they were creating together.

"You feel so damn good," he said, gritting his teeth as he completed another agonizingly good stroke. "It's never… been like this."

"I know," she said, practically sobbing into her hand. "You're so…" She trailed off as he buried himself deep inside her. Too overwhelmed to have any conscious thought at that moment.

"So *what*?" he asked teasingly, his voice raspy with want.

"Never mind. So something I can't think of because you make me feel… too good!" She cried out as he thrust deep within again, feeling a surging pressure rising with each movement in and out. Could she actually go from intercourse? It seemed with Ryder Hart, she could. After a few more intense thrusts, she felt the overwhelming power surge forward within her, shaking her body in a powerful release that had her sobbing at the pleasure that shook her down to her toes. Even her fingertips flooded with pleasure as she dug her nails into his back, wrapping her legs around him to take and hold him deep as she took her release.

He growled her name and held her close, tight, safe, and for the moment, she was in a different world. An animal world where there was only mating and heat and taking and claiming.

She couldn't explain it. It was like the air had changed and her body was responding chemically in ways it never had. As he began to move again, she uttered an oath and held on, savoring the intense feelings he stimulated inside her as she felt the tension in his body building toward his own release. Sensing he couldn't hold on much longer, he moved his hand between them, gently moving over her as he stroked inside. It increased the speed of everything, and she gave herself up to the sensation of pleasure everywhere as a mind-shattering orgasm shook them both.

She treasured the feeling of him shaking inside her as he pumped out his release, and dug her nails in as her own pleasure reverberated inside her in answer to his. She cried out his name and he answered, and they moved together until they were sated and he slumped forward over her body on the couch.

She caught her breath, listening to the pounding of her heart and feeling his heart racing against her. He was still panting with the exertion, and when he lifted his eyes to meet hers, she could tell he was just as shocked, just as satisfied, as she was.

She took a few more deep breaths and waited for her mind to come back to Earth, for reality to settle in. But as she held him and savored the way her body felt after a good loving, she couldn't bring herself to regret what they'd just shared together.

It didn't matter what came after. That was wonderful and always would be.

Ryder snuggled into her and murmured something against her neck. It sounded like, "My mate."

Did she hear that right? That seemed a little odd. But as she stroked his head and felt herself grow sleepy from the orgasms, she decided she must have misheard him.

She'd ask him later. Right now, she needed to sleep and hopefully not have to face the consequences of this for a little while.

CHAPTER
FIVE

RYDER LET HER FALL ASLEEP beneath him, pleased she was sated and seemed happy for the moment. But as his pleasure receded, guilt twisted his stomach. He picked Janna up and carried her to the bedroom they'd be sharing together. He hadn't planned to bring her to his cabin in particular, but he could keep an eye on her better here, in case rival bears got any ideas. He also found himself too jealous at the thought of potentially sharing her company with his brothers or their rowdy friends.

No, for now, Janna was his. And at least for those few moments in his arms, she hadn't seemed to mind. He'd seen the doubt and fear in her melt away, leaving her a supple, beautiful woman open to loving and being loved.

And it had left him breathless.

The bear in him had gone into full-on seduction mode, and he knew no woman could easily resist. At the same time, he'd carefully watched her, not wanting to rush her, not wanting to scare her.

After having her, he was surer than ever.

This was it, his mate. And when he'd blurted that out, she'd given him a weird look. How to explain? *Look, I'm a bear, and we mate for life, usually instinctively when we find our mate, and I want to make you happy forever. Even though I barely know you.*

No. That didn't sound good. He tucked her in and looked at the clock by the bedside. Maybe he should let her sleep while he called Riley. Perhaps Riley had more experience with these things. Ryder had been with women before, sure, but he'd never had this kind of response. This need to claim. He found himself shaken to the core by his reaction to her.

He stepped out of her room and shut the door behind him. Then he pulled on his clothes and got out his cell phone, staring at it pensively.

Cursing himself for not having anyone better to ask, he dialed Riley's number.

No answer. After a few rings, Ryder cursed and hung up. Then he dialed Ryan. It was humiliating to ask this of the youngest brother, but since they were so close in age, it shouldn't be. That's what he told himself. He put a hand to his forehead. He hadn't been planning for things to go this fast.

He'd wanted to have a nice dinner. Maybe make out a little. See where things went. And then his bear had come roaring to life, demanding to take his mate, and she'd been so warm and willing and… well.

But he didn't yet know how she'd react to him being a bear.

Unlike Riley, Ryan picked up promptly.

"Hey." His voice was rough and serious as usual.

Ryder sighed. "Hey."

"Ryder? What's wrong?"

"Nothing," he said quietly, eyeing the bedroom, wondering if Janna could hear him if she woke up. He decided not to take any chances and walked outside the cabin and shut the door behind him. "I may have screwed up."

"Screwed up how? Did you pick up the chick you were interested in?"

"Sort of," he said, ashamed at how nervous, how unsure he sounded. He had ownership in some of the biggest companies in the world, yet he was here, floored because of a beautiful, giving woman that had taken him to heaven when she made love to him.

"What happened? Wait, Riley wants to talk to you. Hold on."

"Bro!" Riley's voice echoed into the mic, and Ryder shook his head and put the earpiece a little ways from his ear.

"Yes."

"Sorry I missed your call. We're having an awesome party in the penthouse up here. You should bring your lady and join."

Ryder gritted his teeth at the thought of her being around that kind of company. "No thanks."

"So what's up? You need my advice with some lady issue?"

Ryder hated that Riley was right with his guess. Ryder liked being in control, being the one who knew what was happening. But how did a responsible person deal with what looked like a one-night stand? What if Janna felt disrespected or pressured? What if she hated him and wanted to go home? How could he explain that he hadn't intended what happened. It had just felt so right. For once, he felt like things had gone very far out of his control. He itched to transform into his bear and run it off, but he knew he couldn't leave his mate here without him to watch out for her.

When he'd been deep inside her, he knew. She had bear blood.

With the promiscuity of wandering male bear shifters and the fact that they'd been increasingly breeding with human women in an attempt to sow wild oats, there had been more and more shifter children born unable to shift but with at least a little shifter blood inside them.

Perhaps that was a little of what had called to him initially about Janna. And her perky, plump breasts, delicious curves, and sassy red lips hadn't helped things. No, he was smitten, and his bear had made up his mind. Whether she could shift or not, she was like him. He'd felt her bear call to his, and they'd nearly mated.

Now he'd protect her with his life, billionaire or not. He just had to figure out how to explain it to her.

"You there?" Riley asked. "Dude, what happened? You sound shaken."

"I… my bear responded to her. She's mine. She has to be."

"Whoa, whoa, whoa," Riley said nervously. "You don't think that stuff about fated mates is just old wives' tales? I mean, supposedly that's how it was with our parents, and look how that worked out."

Ryder frowned. Riley had a point there. What if he changed his mind, turned out like his father? He couldn't hurt Janna like that. But then again, it was his choice, wasn't it?

"You know the best thing for the race is to sow wild oats. It's rare that attempts at reproduction are successful," Riley said.

Ryder frowned. Maybe he didn't care about continuing bear kind. Maybe the lack of monogamy had contributed to the low survival rate of young bears and females. Either way, he was doing it his way or not at all. He wouldn't leave a trail of broken hearts the way his father had.

"Ryder?" Riley asked, perturbed by the silence, as he usually was.

"I think you sow enough wild oats for the rest of us," Ryder said sardonically. "I don't know. I've never wanted someone like I wanted her. We nearly mated. I was ready to claim her."

"You've known her for like a day. Cool it, bro. Maybe you just need more experience with women."

"You'll know it when it happens to you," Ryder replied, rubbing his chest to ease the tension coiling there. "You know what Dad's will said. The heart wants what it wants, and he wishes he had listened. I mean, did Dad have any other offspring with other females? We know he slept around, but he was most successful with our mother and us. I think he realized that near the end of his life. So maybe just one…"

"Whatever floats your boat, dude. Personally, I can't imagine having just one," Riley grumbled, and Ryder heard Ryan scoffing in disgust in the background.

"Look, I didn't come just because of the will. I've gotten where I am in business because I followed my gut. And my gut led me here. And my gut says she's the one."

"Are you sure you aren't just being lazy? Not wanting to look a little harder?" Riley asked doubtfully.

Ryder growled. "I'm sure. Now help me not screw this up."

"Fine, fine. What do you mean screw it up?"

"I slept with her," Ryder said, feeling ashamed even as he said it. He'd never been a man to take advantage or move too quickly. If anything, he'd always been so calculating and slow that sometimes women had given up. And that had been fine, until he met Janna.

It was Scott's fault, he thought grumpily. He'd have had more time to study the proposition of courting Janna if such a persistent rival hadn't been right there, eyeing her like he wanted to eat her up.

But now Ryder had Janna's body, and not her heart, and for all he knew, she'd wake up hating him for disrespecting and seducing her. Though he knew she'd technically been with him every step of the way.

"Yikes," Riley said after a pause. "That's fast. What happened?"

"I don't know. I was just going to kiss her, and then…"

"Then?" Riley sounded altogether too eager, and Ryder bristled.

"None of your business."

"Gotta know the deets if I'm going to help."

"We had sex, okay? Geez."

"Wow, go Ryder. I didn't know you—"

Ryder groaned and put a hand up over his flushed face. "Can you please shut up and tell me what to do now?"

Riley sighed. "Well, she'll want to know it's not some one-time thing and that you don't think differently of her. She'll still want to be wined and dined. I'd order dinner in and talk with her."

"About sex?" Ryder asked.

"No, jackass. About her. Get to know her so when you make your move, she trusts that you really want her for her, you know?"

"You're good at this," Ryder murmured. "Too good. Is there a romance going on that I don't know about?"

There was a pause on Riley's end. "No, just had a few flings. I'm not ready to settle down." Then Riley grumbled something under his breath that Ryder couldn't make out.

"All right. Dinner and talking," Ryder said.

"Right."

"And then?"

"And then let her sleep alone, like a gentleman, and restart things in the morning. You have some time with her, right?"

"Right," he said.

"So yeah, just slow things down again."

"What if I start to, what if my bear…?"

Riley sighed. "Go for a run if you need to. I can keep an eye on your girl. You know now that you're paying attention to her as a grizzly, any smaller bears in the area that couldn't have sensed her before will realize she's a viable mate."

"I know," he says. "But like hell I'm leaving you alone with her."

"Good man," Riley said. "I guess you'll just have to learn to control yourself with her, then."

"Fine," Ryder said, voice sharper than he meant it to be. But the reminder that his interest as a grizzly would perk the interest of other shifters in his potential mate made him as grumpy as his type of bear was purported to be. "I'll call you later. Don't trash the penthouse."

"I'll try," Riley said. "I'm trying to get our little bro to loosen up. I'll let you know how that goes."

Ryder sighed into his hand. "Don't corrupt him, Riley."

Riley just laughed. "We'll see."

Ryder exhaled in frustration as he hung up the call. He paced in front of the door and then heard something smash from inside the cabin. His heart stopped for a second, and then he charged in the front door, worried something had happened to Janna.

He shut the door and stopped dead when he saw her wrapped in a blanket, flushing deeply, standing in the doorway to the bedroom. Her eyes were angry.

Uh-oh.

"Why is your stuff in the closet here?" she asked, anger infusing her tone. "And just what were you planning to do with me?"

CHAPTER
SIX

RYDER LICKED HIS LIPS AND tried to think of a good response. The clock by the bedside was broken at her feet. She must have thrown it.

He knew how it looked. He'd brought her to a cabin and implied it was hers, when all of his stuff was set up in it.

And then he'd bedded her on a couch and been gone when she woke up.

She bit her lip nervously and looked at the clock she'd broken with adorable guilt in her eyes. He couldn't help surveying her generous form and wanting to just take her to bed and make it better, but…

"Were you just thinking I'd be easy?" she asked, brown eyes blazing fire. "I guess I proved you right. You pretend like you want to work together, get me up to your 'cabin,' screw me senseless, and then just get up to take a phone call?"

He winced. How to explain? He was so good at high-pressure negotiation, yet now, with his gorgeous mate spitting all kinds of words that made sense but were totally wrong, he couldn't seem to perform.

"You don't understand," he said, dodging a plate she threw his direction. She was small compared to him, but damn did she scare him. Still, he'd expect nothing less from his strong-minded potential mate. "I wasn't planning that. I was just as taken aback as you were. It's been a long time since I've... been with someone. Dated someone. You were... irresistible."

Her expression softened, but her lips stayed pressed together. "You expect me to believe Ryder Hart just couldn't control himself with me?"

"There's more to it," Ryder said nervously, scrubbing the back of his neck with one hand and wondering what to do about the bear thing. "I just... can't explain it all yet. How about we have dinner?"

Her eyes flashed, but just then, her stomach made a betraying growling noise.

"I promise that won't happen again," he said. "Unless you want it. Even then, we'd have to talk first. Despite what it looks like, that's not what I want from you, Janna. I know this sounds crazy, but I want you. Just as you are."

"You barely know me," she said darkly.

"Do you believe in love at first sight?" he tried weakly.

"No," she said.

He sighed. If he didn't have his bear, he wouldn't either. But he knew his animal had wisdom about this that he didn't. He would trust it and hope it would lead him to the right way to win her.

"Give me a chance," he said. "Let's try and put this behind us for now." She blushed, and he swallowed, trying to press on despite the delicious thoughts of her that kept coming to his head. Janna writhing beneath him, Janna moaning his name, Janna crying out for him, and his bear answering…

"Just give me the week you were going to give me," he said. "Forgive me for this mistake."

Her eyes flashed in anger, and he realized that was a bad way to word it.

"No," he corrected. "I mean…" The stubborn part of him had enough. "Woman, I'm getting dinner. And you're going to eat that and then listen to what I have to say." He eyed her sternly, hoping that sent the right message.

Instead, she looked at him for a moment and then burst into laughter. Then she sashayed away into the bedroom.

Suddenly, Ryder wasn't sure who was in control after all. Damn. His mate was a one-in-a-million woman.

JANNA SANK AGAINST THE DOOR, grateful she'd had a chance to shut it in Ryder's face before her mocking laughter turned into something more hysterical. She covered her mouth with her hand, waiting for her heartbeat to return to normal.

Even angry with him for leaving her alone in bed, even yelling at him for bringing her to his cabin and not telling her, he had an effect on her.

Tall, handsome Ryder Hart was just as devastatingly gorgeous when he was hemming and hawing over making a mistake as he was when he was making love to her.

A deep part of her said, *Let's keep him.*

Another part said, *We've been wrong before. He could leave us. We have no promise of anything.* And to be fair, when she made love to him, she hadn't demanded anything but the pleasure he could give her. She had no right to be angry with him for something that had been her choice.

But that was when she'd thought he'd been just as carried away as she was. Heck, she'd only been alone with him for two minutes before she practically jumped his bones. Gone was the practical accountant; in her place was a feral animal eager to get any piece of him.

It wasn't like her. She rubbed her chest over her heart, still not feeling fully like herself. Perhaps it was just the sex, but she still felt exhilarated. More alive than ever before.

And damn, could he do sex.

But then she'd seen the clothes in the closet. He hadn't changed his mind and brought her to her own private cabin, as she'd initially thought. He'd brought her to *his* place, like a presumptuous first date who assumed he was going to get some. Worse, she'd proven him right.

But even as her logical mind chastised her for her indiscretion, her body ached with relief that they'd been together. It had felt wonderful, been exactly what she needed, and he'd used protection. So what was the harm?

She wasn't old-fashioned enough to feel that it should affect his opinion of her. And yet, she still wanted him to know she didn't just jump into bed with every hot billionaire that wanted her.

Crazy as it sounded, there had been something between them. Something she wanted to explore, even though she knew better than to hope for something to happen this quickly with one of the most powerful men in the country.

Ryder Hart. *Ryder Hart* had been making love to her. She could barely believe it.

He was waiting out there. She giggled again at his attempt to be commanding. Sure, it had made her go weak in the knees. But she also knew now she had equal, or maybe more, power over him now. His attempt to command her had simply stemmed from his adorable sense of frustration at the situation. And looking at his crumpled brow, rumpled clothing, and huge muscles that could nonetheless not get him out of this mess, she couldn't fight back a laugh.

And it had felt good and made her feel more in control of a situation that had started to worry her.

She wasn't going to fall too hard for Ryder Hart. Not more than she wanted to. She'd taken what she wanted, no more, and as she heard him out and got to know him, maybe she'd be more able to decide what she wanted from him.

She grinned and opened her suitcase, looking for something to torture him. She heard his low, sexy voice on the phone, probably ordering dinner, and lust coiled inside her again. *No*, she told her body, *we're not doing that again. Not soon. We need to get to know him. See if we can trust him.*

You can, a part of her said. But she ignored it. She needed more than intuition this time. It was too easy to mistake intuition for simply something she wanted anyway. She wouldn't be fooled again.

And with a man who could have any choice of woman on his arm, she'd have to be extra careful if she didn't want to end up cheated on again.

She put on a bra that pushed the ladies up and together in a pleasing way, pulled on some Spanx that smoothed from the bottom of her breasts to her knees, and put on a soft V-neck sweater in red and a form-fitting black skirt. She gave her hair a quick toss, knowing there was nothing much she could do for the tight, unruly curls, and swiped on her signature red lipstick.

Her pretty brown skin didn't need makeup, still glowing from sex, so she crossed through the room and opened the door to peek out shyly.

Though she was pretty sure she was a knockout in this outfit, she couldn't help feeling a shudder of self-consciousness when she met his sapphire-blue gaze. His full lips pressed into a firm line, and she thought she saw him shift slightly, as if he were instantly aroused by her. She pushed away the thought and swept into the room and headed for a cupboard. She pulled out a mug and filled it with ice water from the fridge and sat down at the table to look out the window at the snow as if nothing were wrong.

Ryder let out a little huff and sat across from her. There was silence for a moment, and she could tell it bothered him more than it bothered her. So she sipped her water annoyingly and waited for him to say something. It was more entertaining that way.

"I was thinking we could head up to the lodge at eight in the morning tomorrow. Get started on the books."

"Mm-hmm," she said, not looking at him.

He cleared his throat. Even that sound was enough to send shockwaves down to her toes. "Does that sound okay? And then I arranged for a special lunch."

She turned to him. "Special?"

It was his turn to grin slyly, a knowing look in those beautiful eyes. He brushed dark hair off his forehead. "You'll see. I want it to be a surprise."

She shrugged. "I guess so. After tonight, that's some big shoes to fill."

He coughed. "Excuse me?"

She laughed, trying to hide her nerves at blurting that out. "I just mean, after what happened this evening, it'll be difficult to surprise me."

"Oh," he said simply, sounding baffled. "Well, I hope this surprise is better."

"That'd be hard," she retorted.

He shifted in his chair and she stifled a laugh by putting her water to her lips again.

"Well, we'll see," he said. "Anyway, I ordered dinner. I hope you like steak."

"Who doesn't?" she said glibly. The longer she was near him, the more nervous she felt, even when she wasn't looking at him.

"The lodge restaurant has been impressive so far. And I told them it was a special occasion. I expect they won't disappoint."

"When will they be coming?"

"Ten minutes or so," he said. "It took you a few minutes to get ready. Not that I mind." His eyes ran over her slowly, taking in every inch like he wanted to strip the clothing right off of her and start all over again.

She wriggled in her chair, a little uncomfortable in the Spanx. He eyed her midsection, as if he could tell something wasn't quite right, but then decided not to say anything about it.

"So tell me about you, Janna. Despite my rather rude attempts so far, I really do want to get to know you. I promise."

She sighed. "All right. Since I have nothing else to do right now, I'll give you a chance. I mean, I have to say, what we just did? I'd be lying if I didn't say it blew my mind."

"I'm glad," he said, and the warmth was back between them, melting away the awkwardness like sun on spring snow. "It blew my mind, too."

"What do you want to know?"

"What are your hopes and dreams?" he asked, leaning forward on his impressive forearms. "What do you want more than anything in the world?"

Safety, she thought to herself. *A little place with someone I can trust, who sees me for who I am, and who accepts me and would never leave.*

But didn't every woman want that? The fairytale? She could take care of herself; she knew that. But she still wanted a partner who could do it for her sometimes. When she was tired. Someone she could care for too.

But looking into Ryder's handsome, striking face, she couldn't say it.

"I guess I'd like to own my own business. Pay the mortgage off, you know?"

"Would you want to stay here in town if you did?"

She shrugged. "Depends who is here." She blushed because she knew that was too obvious. If Ryder Hart settled here, then yes, she'd be tempted to stay. That is if things worked out between them. Which she knew she was crazy to hope for. "I'd like to be independent. And at some point, I guess I would like a family."

"Kids?" he asked.

"Sure," she said.

"How many?"

"I don't know," she said. "The biological clock is ticking. I don't think I'd mind adopting though."

He winced. "You're still in your prime."

"You have something against adoption?"

He shook his head, his thick, dark hair moving in tantalizing ways around his face and neck. "No, I just hate seeing you think you're too old to have your own if you want to. I think adoption is amazing."

She smiled because she could see he was being genuine. For some reason, he didn't seem like the type to lie. Maybe the type to put his foot in it by telling too much truth too fast, but not a snake like Scott.

Even if she did get the feeling Ryder was hiding something. Then again, they barely knew each other. It was natural to keep some things hidden.

At least that's what she told herself.

"So your friends. Tell me about them," he said.

"My friends?"

"Yeah, the girls you were with when I first met you. Seems like you've found something good there," he said.

She warmed at the fact that he'd been paying attention. One of the things she'd always hated about Scott was how he didn't seem to listen or notice little things that were important to her. "Well, I guess that's one thing I should be grateful to Scott for. Without him, I wouldn't have met Kylie or Leslie. They've made all the difference in my life."

"I'd say that's because you made all the difference in theirs, not because of any virtue of Scott's." He frowned, and she could swear the big man was pouting. The thought made her heart skip a beat. If he were just a one-night stand looking for a local girl to romance for a week, would he look that jealous whenever Scott's name was brought up?

"Still, I never would have met them if I hadn't gone to Leslie's bar, trying to drown my sorrows. And Kylie has her own story."

"They're both locals?" Ryder asked, seeming genuinely interested in a way that made her warm inside.

"Yes," she said. "And they've been a huge blessing. I wish they could come up here."

"You could invite them," he said. But he seemed to regret that the moment it was out of his mouth, and she was glad. Because as much as she loved seeing her friends, she couldn't resist the thought of just a little more time with Ryder Hart. All to herself. She could castigate herself afterwards for being stupid about it.

For now, she wanted the fantasy.

And even if it went bad, wouldn't she have the most amazing story to tell?

"Now, how about you?" she asked, turning the empty mug in her hands. "What are your hopes and dreams, Ryder Hart?"

When he grinned at her and started to speak, she found herself simultaneously second-guessing herself and falling in love with him.

Ryder Hart was indeed going to be trouble.

CHAPTER
SEVEN

"I WANT TO MAKE A difference in the world," he said, and Janna's heart gave a nervous little double thump.

"Yes, I got that about you when you came up with the locals-only discount idea."

He eyed her narrowly, as if trying to decide if she was making fun of him or not, and then relaxed. "I know it sounds odd. The consummate capitalist caring about something like that. But I want to leave a legacy."

"What about children?" she asked, fingering the lip of her mug pensively.

"What about them?"

"Won't that be your legacy?"

He bit his full lower lip and she crossed her legs to hide the effect it had on her. For some reason, he seemed nervous about the topic of children. "I do hope to have kids. But I also hope to leave a better world for them. And to change the lives of other kids."

"I *had* heard Ryder Hart was big into philanthropy," she said quietly, not knowing where to push forward or pull back with the big, quiet man. Sometimes, he could be so forceful and intimidating and other times, so thoughtful and drawn in on himself.

"I am. Because I've been given much, I too must give."

"Well, given and earned."

"Same thing," he said. "There are people who work just as hard as I do and don't make the same. That makes me feel responsible to even the stakes."

"How?"

"Donations. Building shelters for the less fortunate. Sponsoring foreign aid programs. I could go on and on, but the list would bore you."

"I thought you were just trying to impress me," she said with a warm, knowing smile.

He grinned and leaned back in his chair. "Is it working?"

"Yes," she said. "Especially since I can just get online and Google you if I need to verify anything."

"I suppose so. Though you won't get internet out here. I'd need to take you up to the lodge." He cocked his head and a dark lock caressed his forehead. She had the oddest urge to reach over and tuck it back out of the way. It was a crime to hide any of that beautiful, smooth skin. He had lines, sure, but they were the type that added character, at the corner of his eyes and faintly at the side of his mouth. He looked like a man in the prime of his life who had lived enough to be interesting.

Had she lived enough to be interesting? She sort of hoped they didn't have to talk about her career. Accounting wasn't exactly an exciting topic.

A knock on the door sounded, and Ryder stood smoothly to answer. He exchanged words and possibly a tip with whomever was there and then came back with takeout bags in his hand that were emitting steam and a wonderful smell.

"That smells amazing," she said as he pulled clean dishes from the cupboard and started setting the table. It was easy for him to reach even the top shelves of everything, and Janna thought it would be nice to have him around. She wouldn't have to always be grabbing the footstool to get things in her kitchen.

Well, her foolish brain could think of a lot of reasons he'd be great to have around. But fairytales just didn't happen. She needed to remember that and keep her eye on the prize. The pay that would get her out of here and help her forget the mistake she made with Scott forever.

But she felt just a tinge of longing that it could be different. That someone like she and Ryder really could fit together.

"I was hoping to cook for you, but after…" He trailed off, flushing adorably, and started taking out large takeout containers to serve onto the plates. "Well, we'll do it when you're less tired. I'm sure you're starving."

She was about to protest but remembered her stomach rumbling.

"I promise you can count on me to be more of a gentleman," he said, pushing her plate toward her. A deep-brown steak emitting savory fumes was laid alongside grilled asparagus. A meal that would be filling and healthy at the same time. And indulgent. How long had it been since she went out?

She waited for him to be served and then noticed him waiting for her to take a bite. She eyed him suspiciously, not liking being watched when eating.

"Ah, sorry," he said, averting his eyes and taking a bite. "I'm afraid one of my failings is I sort of prefer my women well fed."

"Well, we are less grumpy that way," she said lightly, cutting into her steak.

"That's not why… Oh, never mind."

She chewed a bite of her meat, intrigued enough that she barely tasted it. "What do you mean that's not why? Why, then?"

He gritted his teeth and she definitely thought she could make out a light flush on his high, severe cheekbones. She'd embarrassed Ryder Hart somehow. "I… Well, I'll explain more later. I've already messed things up enough today."

"So you like women with a little meat on their bones," she said, happily working her way through the meal as they spoke. The awkwardness of the moment wasn't enough to counteract the tastiness of the entree. "Nothing to be ashamed of there."

"I said I didn't want to talk about it," he said quietly, continuing to eat. "But yes, short story, I like it. Now eat."

"I am," she said, grinning. "So what are you going to cook for me later?"

He perked up at that and set down his fork. He didn't seem very hungry. More nervous. "Whatever you like. What are your favorites?"

"Whatever you want to cook," she said.

"Easy to please. I like that."

"Do you?" she asked, eyes flashing to his. "I sort of got the impression you liked hard to get."

He met her gaze with hard sapphire blue. "Are you hard to get?"

She didn't blink. "Maybe."

"Then, yes, I like it," he said, leaning back in his chair and eyeing her with that strangely predatory yet flattering gaze.

She finished her meal as they spoke about their families. Ryder wouldn't say much other than he and his brothers left home for school and hadn't been back, and rarely saw one another but kept in touch. Janna could tell him most of the truth about her family. Controlling mom, gorgeous, skinny sister whom she was relieved Ryder didn't seem at all interested in meeting, and a father who worked too much and wasn't really around.

Perhaps she hadn't dated around enough before Scott, and that's why she fell the way she did. And perhaps her dad hadn't been around enough to teach her anything about men.

And perhaps, with how cruel life had been to her at times, she simply didn't want to overthink things when life was actually good. It felt fair that life would be good for once. That's why it was so awful when things with Scott went bad.

But it did leave her here, away from her family, where she could grow as a person and meet people like Ryder. And Leslie and Kylie. She wondered if her friends were trying to figure out how to get into the parties at the lodge. Maybe she should mention something to get them an in next time she saw Ryder's brothers.

Not that she knew when that would be. He tended to be tense and a little cagey when it came to talking about other men, as if he were jealous but knew he had no right to be this early in the game. But to be honest, it made her feel safe. Protected. She knew that someone who was his would never worry about being treasured. And she was strong enough to stand up for herself if someone were acting controlling.

After all, she hadn't hesitated to laugh in his face when he'd tried it before. Caveman dominance was fun in the bedroom, but out of it, she was a grown woman and expected to be treated like one.

"Where have you gone in your mind?" Ryder's voice cut into her thoughts. "Don't get me wrong. I kind of love that about you already. But I find myself wishing I could go with you."

She flushed with warmth. That was one of the nicest things anyone had said to her. Not telling her to come back or chiding her for not paying attention or telling her not to zone out. Just wishing he could go with her.

She tried to keep her heart from melting on the spot. "Just thinking about family. And life. And you know, the things that get you where you are."

"Tell me about it," he said. "I was dreading this trip and the memories it would bring. And then I laid eyes on you and knew everything happens for a reason."

"How can you be so sure? You barely know me."

"You keep saying that, and I keep trying to answer it. I can't explain it other than to say I don't do this with everyone. Anyone even. Just you. You're special."

She poked the remains of her dinner around with her fork. "It's not that I don't want to believe you. It's just hard to."

"I know. That's why we've got a week," he said, finishing his dinner. When she nodded at him, he took both plates and put them in the sink and started running water.

"You wash dishes too?" she asked.

"Yup," he said with a grin. "Fully housebroken."

"Nice," she said. "Definitely points in your favor."

He gave her a slightly predatory grin that was playful nonetheless. "I'll make sure to redeem them later."

The mood changed, and he seemed aware he'd done it. "Well, I'll redeem them by letting you cook for me."

She tried not to be disappointed. What could she say, that she'd hoped they could be redeemed in somewhat… sexier ways? She'd sound stupid being the only one thinking that. He was determined to behave himself. Why couldn't she do the same?

Except, they were both consenting adults. Why couldn't they have a little fun? Well, for the sake of the slight soreness between her legs, she'd follow her logical side and let things cool off for tonight. But she couldn't help feeling a little snuggly, with her stomach full and the cabin so warm and an hour of great conversation with a good-looking man.

Ryder wouldn't let her finish the dishes, so she turned on the big-screen in the living room and watched reality TV while she waited.

When he came and sat down next to her, the air heated a couple degrees. He was just so damn big she wanted to just cuddle back against him. She'd fit right against that wide chest.

Luckily, he seemed to have the same idea because he pulled her close and wrapped an arm around her waist. She squirmed because the odd angle wasn't comfortable with the Spanx. He ran a hand along her middle and then frowned.

"You should go take those off. You deserve to be comfortable. Also, let it be known that from here on out, whatever that thing is hiding, I would rather see."

She frowned, not liking being told what to do, but when he pulled away from her, waiting for her to change, she sighed and gave in. It wasn't like she wanted to stay uncomfortable. But there was a still a part of her that felt she had to strap herself in or minimize her fat to be loved. She was one half loving her body and one half afraid that anyone else hating it could break her fragile self-esteem.

She stood and went into the bedroom to change. She decided she might as well put him to the full test of how comfortable he liked her, so she changed into comfy, loose black workout pants that flattered her rear and a soft hooded sweatshirt in a flattering shade of pink.

His eyes warmed when he saw her, and she blushed in response. She knew she was acting like a sixteen-year-old on her first date, but she couldn't help it. This was the most exciting thing to happen to her in a long time. And she needed lots of good tidbits to pass on to Leslie and Kylie so they could live vicariously.

"I wish my friends could see this," she said. "It's beautiful up here."

He straightened as she sat, and then pulled her in against him to cuddle. He leaned over her hair. "You smell wonderful."

"Um, thanks," she said with a laugh. She inhaled his musky scent. Pine and forest and cold rivers. "You do too."

"Thank you." He smoothed his arm along her middle. "Much better. So soft."

"Hey, no creeping," she said, wriggling away. "And no touching my fat."

"I'm touching you, not your fat. And if you don't like it, I'll stop." He started to pull back, but she grabbed his arms and tugged them around her. They were huge, protective, and warm. No way she was giving them up.

Only problem was they made her think of earlier in the evening and what they'd done on the couch they were now sitting on. Damn.

"As for your friends, you're welcome to call them up. As for sleeping arrangements, I didn't mean to bring you to my cabin. It's just when I thought about subjecting you to the parties at the lodge, and my brothers, I wanted to give you something private. You can take the bedroom, and I'll take the couch. You can also call the girlfriends over and share the cabin with them."

"Where would you go?"

"I'd still be here."

"Um, no offense, but I don't think they're going to want to stay here with a dude in the living room."

He frowned. "I didn't think of that."

"You didn't think this through much, did you?"

"Honestly, I thought of it all on the spot when I saw you in that store and saw that Scott creep getting ready to make his move."

She gave him a surprised look, then shrugged. "Well, I guess if it's that short notice, you didn't do too badly after all."

"Glad you think so," he said, holding her tight.

She held back a long sigh. He was so warm, so right. She wanted to stay here watching trashy TV while snow fell and just forget that life existed outside. She also wanted to take him back to the bedroom and make him prove what they'd had wasn't a one-time thing. Already, her body was aching for more. She'd never been like that with Scott, never felt this constant, bone-weary need for him.

She didn't think she was the type to be swayed by Ryder's fame or reputation, so she wasn't sure exactly what it was. Maybe it was just him. Maybe you really could get to know someone quickly if they were open enough.

Or maybe she was just letting her heart do more dangerous wishful thinking.

When it was dark outside, she said good night and reluctantly pulled herself out of his arms. He insisted he could set himself up on the couch and didn't even go to the closet in her room. Instead, he pulled out a travel suitcase from a closet by the door. Ryder Hart was apparently the type who prepared for anything.

She watched him making up his bed on the couch and leaned against the frame of her bedroom door. She was surprised by the feeling of tenderness that hit her as she watched the big man trying to get comfortable on the too-small sleeping space.

Invite him in, a part of her said.

Not yet, the more persuasive part answered.

And because she'd already listened to the first part and done something far outside of her comfort zone, she allowed herself to stay inside her comfort zone on this. She bid him good night and shut the door.

But the look in his sapphire eyes stayed with her for hours before she fell asleep and then visited in her dreams, which were oddly about bears in the woods.

So when she woke to see a pair of plaintive bear eyes staring at her, she at first thought she was dreaming. But a minute later, when she realized she was all too awake, she let out a blood-shattering scream.

CHAPTER
EIGHT

RYDER JUMPED ON THE COUCH where he was sleeping and rubbed his eyes. Something had woken him. A scream. Had he imagined it? He leaned forward, listening keenly in the direction of Janna's room.

Another scream rang out, and he ran off the couch, dragging his blanket with him, and strode to her door. He knocked hurriedly, and when she didn't respond immediately, he barged in.

She turned to him with tear-stained eyes, and he felt his heart clench in his chest. So this was the effect of a mate. He'd thought his heart was going to stop when he heard her scream. He let out a breath and walked over to her bed. She was staring mutely at the window, pointing with a shaking hand.

"Bear," she muttered. "I saw a bear. I swear it."

He bit his lip. "What kind of bear?"

"It was black," she said.

He sighed with relief. He could take on any black bear that got ideas. He could take on any grizzly as well, but it'd be more complicated. Luckily, he expected he and his brothers were the only ones in the area with grizzly blood. But bear shifters could mate interspecies, and with him awakening the more animal side of her, he should have expected that bears would already be circling. He would probably have to shift into bear form to patrol at nights. He'd prefer sleeping here in her room to watch her, but she didn't seem to trust him that far yet. And also, if he had to shift, she'd see him. And he didn't know how to explain that yet.

He sat on the bed and put an arm out, and she cuddled under it. Damn, he loved the feel of her feminine, warm body under his. Every bear he knew loved ladies with curves. Not that other ladies weren't fine, but there was something about a lady with extra that made him feel more secure. It probably had something to do with bears in the wild and reproductive rates. He thought he recalled his father saying something to that effect, that female bears without the right amount of extra weight couldn't get pregnant.

But right now, he didn't care about getting Janna pregnant. He could cross that bridge when he came to it. Right now, he cared about making her feel safe again.

He needed her to feel safe as much as he needed to breathe.

"Shh... it's okay. Tell me what happened, from the beginning."

She sniffed and took a deep breath, and he felt her grow stronger in his arms. He loved that about her. She didn't just keel over and let life walk on her. But that didn't stop a fierce protective instinct from rising in him and making itself known. "I had weird dreams last night. About bears, for some reason."

He swallowed. Should he tell her now? Would she run screaming? He'd always avoided women for just this reason. If there had been a bear shifter female around who could shift, it would have been easier to explain. But how did he explain it to someone who was mostly human? And once he did, how did he keep her from thinking he only meant to breed her? It was complicated being part human, part animal.

"Anyway, when I woke up, these dark, almost black eyes were staring at me. Staring straight into me. And I had the evilest feeling when I looked into them. I felt—and this sounds crazy, I know—but I felt it *wanted* me."

He gritted his teeth and suppressed a growl. Yes, he supposed the bear *would* want her, with her curves, her strong spirit, everything he liked about her.

Only one problem, she was *his*. Once he'd claimed her in the way bears claimed mates, the other bears would know she was taken and back off. But until then...

Bears weren't like wolf shifters, who were more common and marked their mates merely through unprotected sex and mutual orgasm. The bear claiming ritual was more complicated and frankly, a little odd and not something one could just pull off without explaining. Not that he'd ever do that to an innocent woman.

But how to explain?

She snuggled into him. "Anyway, I'm glad you're here." She let out a dry laugh. "I still can't believe I'm here with Ryder Hart."

And I can't believe I'm here with a warm, loving dream of a woman who is perfect in every way except not knowing I can turn into an animal.

Still, Ryder knew he'd shift if he needed to protect her. He'd do it without thinking and without caring if she hated him after for hiding his secret. The thought of any harm coming to her was unacceptable. Every minute with her made him more unwilling to picture life without her.

It made life back in Silicon Valley seem too empty. Maybe it was time to retire. Travel. Keep up the philanthropy but live off the proceeds of his investments.

He nuzzled his mate's head, comfortable with calling her that now. No, he'd probably always be a shark in business, but with Janna, his life could be more balanced. Maybe they could spend part of the year here, maybe in San Diego, where she was from...

He realized she was stirring against him nervously and wondered what he should say now. *Marry me? I know it's only been a day or two, but I'm certain we could spend our lives having fun together?*

No, that wouldn't work.

"I'll go check outside the cabin," he said, standing. But she tugged on his sleeve.

"No, don't go out there. He could be out there still."

"I have bear spray," he said.

She kept her hold on his sleeve, and he was amused by her protectiveness of him. "No, just wait. How about we get ready for work and head out together. You wanted to get an early start on the paperwork, right?"

"Right," he said, impressed once again by her bravery. She wanted to come with him. She was one in a million. He'd been right to listen to his bear. "Well, I'll get dressed, then. Will you feel safe in here? I can turn around and cover my eyes."

She laughed, a low, sultry sound that had his groin tightening in response. "No, I'll be fine. But if you did stay, I think covering your eyes would be beyond the point. Considering what we did."

He groaned. "Don't remind me."

She laughed again and shooed him out, and he let out a long sigh as he pulled clothing from his travel bag. He was halfway dressed with no shirt when she came out, her hair in a tight ponytail with wispy curls escaping at the front in an adorable way. He froze, shirt over his head, and watched her gaze travel down his abdomen.

He was proud as she studied him. As a bear shifter, and a grizzly at that, his physique was matchless. Naturally muscled and buff with great tone. Rare for someone his height who was not a shifter. At 6'7", Ryder was a force to be reckoned with, cashmere sweater or no. And he liked that he knew he was capable of protecting her from almost anything in the world. Anything on legs, that was.

Her pretty brown skin flushed and she looked away, seeming like it was hard for her to do. He bit back a grin. His mate liked the way he looked. Perfect. He pulled on his favorite sweater. A deep emerald green that reminded him of runs in the forest. He did up his belt and put on shoes and socks while she did up her coat. His mate looked gorgeous today, in red again. A red sweater with dark, tight jeans that drew attention to each little curve of her luscious body.

Ryder hoped it wasn't obvious that his mouth was watering. She walked over to him, and he found himself once again appreciating her height. If she hadn't been somewhat tall for a woman, it would have been more difficult for him to kiss and hold her. He liked that there was enough of her to feel bountiful and luxurious in his arms. Though he had a feeling that if he'd met her any other way at any other weight, he still would have been smitten.

It was what she had inside her as well. That obvious integrity and that infallible independence that inexplicably made him want to take care of her.

There was something satisfying about a woman who was able to live without you but wanted to live with you.

He grinned as he followed her out to the truck. Even in her long trench coat, he could see her large ass swaying tantalizingly, and he adjusted the front of his pants to be less painful when he was sure she wasn't looking. His inner bear stayed on the lookout, scenting the air for any hint of a competing predator. He was uneasy about the black bear.

But black bear shifters were just so submissive compared to grizzlies. He really wouldn't have to worry until one of those set their sights on Janna. And if either of his brothers did, he'd slap them silly.

But he couldn't forget Janna saying how evil it had felt to look into the bear's eyes. It kept him slightly off balance on the entire walk to the lodge. He smiled and listened with one ear as Janna laid out her plans for going over the books for the lodge, but he couldn't seem to stop thinking about the fact that someone had come to scare his mate when she'd been under his protection.

His protection. Neither his grizzly nor his human was accustomed to people daring to mess with things that were his. And now that he had someone who meant more than anything, he didn't like that it was happening now.

"You okay?" she asked. "You look tense."

"I'm fine," he said. "I'm glad the bear seems to be gone. Honestly, he was probably just drawn by the food and scared off by your scream."

"That's true," she said. "He seemed just as startled by my yelling as I was by him being there when I woke up."

"Creeper bear," Ryder muttered.

"Creepbear?" she said, putting the two words together.

He laughed and put an arm around her and was happy when she didn't resist. He really had no right to, especially when they were about to go in under the guise of merely working together, but he couldn't help wanting at least to show some possession before they encountered other men, like his brothers.

Speak of the devils, Riley and Ryan were standing by the front desk. Riley was flirting shamelessly with a blushing front desk lady, and Ryan was studying his nails, looking bored. Then again, if Ryan wasn't outside having some kind of sporting adventure, he was always bored.

Ryder drew himself to full height, trying to look intimidating as they approached. He could feel the pheromones from his future mate and knew his brothers would be aware of it. Sure enough, Riley looked up with a grin in those keen hazel eyes that had won so many women's hearts and stared from Janna to Ryder with a look that said he knew exactly what was going on. Ryan looked up long enough to give a nod, scent the air, and then go back to whatever game he was messing around with on his phone.

"You guys gonna go over the books?" Riley asked. He stepped forward and held out a hand to Janna. She took it, and he was about to bring it to his lips to kiss it when Ryder swatted a hand between them, breaking contact.

"Yes. What are you two up to today?" he asked, hoping his stern tone implied as severely as possible that they should make themselves scarce.

Riley's grin only deepened at his brother's serious expression. "I'm thinking about hitting the slopes, letting Ryan teach me something."

"He has a crush on one of the lift operators," Ryan muttered.

"Do not," Riley said, pouting. Riley may have been in his mid-twenties, but sometimes it seemed like fame had kept him in suspended animation as a teenager. But then, at other times, he could be almost too serious and prone to depression. And that's when he tended to fly out to Ryder to recover and get some privacy. They'd watch Ryan doing whatever sport he was doing and talk about the old days.

Except for some things. Some things from the old days they never talked about.

Like how their dad had started ignoring them and how their mother had died alone on an icy road.

Riley tapped him on the shoulder, winked at Janna, and dragged Ryan off by the elbow.

Supposedly, a lift operator was about to have a much more difficult day. Riley knew his exact effect on women and enjoyed flustering them. Ryder didn't get it. He wanted Janna to be comfortable with him. Happy. Not jostled.

He waved at Riley and Ryan as they left and turned to the front desk lady, who was staring after them and patting her hair back into its bun.

"How have things been this morning, Amanda?"

"Good," she said, blushing and looking embarrassed to have been caught off guard. She was married with two kids and lived in an apartment here at the lodge. Did Riley have no shame? "Anything I can get for you this morning?"

"No," he said, glad he had such a capable woman serving as front desk help as well as concierge. "Just taking Janna back to look at the books."

The woman appraised Janna with a knowing look and a slight smile. "Of course. Janna's the best around. I never did get why your father insisted on Barry." She stuck out her tongue in disgust and opened the gate to let them back behind the desk.

"Me neither," Ryder said, patting the woman's shoulder as he walked by. "But then, there's a lot I don't understand about the old man."

Amanda unlocked the door behind her for them and Ryder led Janna through.

"Thanks, Amanda. If you could make sure we're not disturbed?"

She winked and motioned zipping her lips. "Mum's the word."

He smiled. He liked Amanda. He'd only known her a couple of days, but they'd had an understanding between them almost from the moment they met.

Ryder considered himself a good judge of people. He tended to decide whether he liked someone within moments of meeting them, and that tended not to change. He guessed it was the bear in him, making decisions based on scent and instinct as to trustworthiness. But it had never led him astray so far.

When he led Janna to the files, she was all business, impressing him again in yet another way. Her sharp eyes scoured the record keeping and she pushed red-lined papers his way as she explained what she saw. The embezzlement was worse than he'd thought. Still, he was sure the betrayal would have hurt his father more than losing the actual money.

For all he knew, his father knew Barry was embezzling and let the man do it. He knew his father could be kindhearted at times. Like when he paid for their college or started them all with a nest egg to begin their careers. He, Riley, and Ryan would never have been as easily able to slip into their new lives without that help. They all still would have made it in the end, but it would have been slower, more difficult, and so he felt he owed his father something.

He'd owe him even more if things worked out with Janna. They worked for hours, solving issues and making plans. Janna's brain was really something to watch. He could only imagine how much she'd be able to do given his finances. He could easily see her overseeing the philanthropy in particular. She'd seemed excited by that.

As for him, he was excited each time she tucked a little wayward curl behind her ear. She seemed to have an endless amount of hair, and a bit was always trying to escape. He wanted to touch her hair, but he knew it would be too hard to resist trailing his hand farther down, over those velvet lips, to the tops of her full breasts…

Damn, working with her was going to be harder than he thought.

Literally.

CHAPTER
NINE

JANNA TRIED TO STAY FOCUSED on the papers, but she felt too painfully aware that Ryder seemed to want to eat her up. His gaze was intense, admiring, as he watched her work through the numbers, and she hoped she wasn't messing anything up.

She set aside the sheet she'd most recently finished and stretched, not missing Ryder's gaze flicking to her chest, which pressed against her tight sweater. She grinned. "So I think that's all I can take of numbers right now. How about that special lunch you promised me?"

His deep-blue eyes widened slightly, and he nodded and straightened up. She returned the favor of checking him out while he stretched. His pecs were enormous, cut in that perfect, square shape she liked so much.

"Well, if you want to wait here for a few moments, I just need to get a few things together."

She nodded at him and picked up a packet of papers she might as well start looking at. Dang, Barry had left things a mess for her. Then again, Barry probably wasn't planning on anyone looking at these anytime soon. To be honest, she wasn't sure what he'd planned to do when Royce died. He had to know his sons, one of whom happened to be extremely financially successful, would want to take a look at the business they'd be inheriting.

It was odd that Royce had never mentioned his sons. She'd been here at the lodge for some of his parties, always low key, but never heard him mention his family. She'd always just assumed he was an old bachelor and never thought to ask Leslie or Kylie about it.

The door shut behind Ryder and she sighed and rolled her shoulders, relieved at the lack of sexual tension. Being in the same room with him, even looking at financials, was exhausting. Something inside her kept urging her closer, telling her to take a chance on this mysterious, powerful man.

But that stubborn part of her (that was, she supposed, her mother talking) that wanted her to stay safe wouldn't shut up long enough for her lustful thoughts to continue unabated. So she kept fighting them, and she was feeling physically tired from it.

The odd dreams and waking up half scared to death by the bear didn't help.

But the bear's eyes. They'd been so odd, almost... human? Somewhat familiar, but she didn't know how.

Her phone buzzed and she realized she hadn't checked messages since yesterday. She opened it and let her voicemails play on speaker.

Not too much of note. Sherry had left a message saying everything was good at the store and she would be missed. Her mother sent a message asking if she knew where her sister was. She shook her head at that. Beth liked to use the money from her various alimony payments to travel. Janna couldn't be expected to keep track of that.

The last message made her pause and then made a slow tremor of fear work its way down her spine.

"Think you're pretty smart? If I were you, I'd leave the lodge."

The voice was low, ominous. At first, she thought of Scott, but then she shook away that thought. It was too aggressive for him. He liked to intimidate in different ways, and he'd never outright threatened her. Just been overly available.

Her finger paused over the play button, shaking slightly as she tried to decide whether or not to replay it.

Then Ryder walked in, excitement on his handsome face and snow lightly dusting his hair, like he'd been outside. "They're here. Let's go."

"Who's here?" she asked, slipping her phone in her pocket and making a mental note to think about mentioning the message to Ryder later. Nothing could happen to her as long as she was with him anyway.

"The surprise." His face was boyishly mischievous, but his body was all man as he helped her on with her coat and ushered her out of the back room. "Come with me."

She had no choice but to follow him, yanked along by her arm entwined through his, though his stride was much faster and longer than hers. Tall men. Sigh.

He practically lifted her up the stairs to the top floor and then unlocked a door she hadn't noticed behind some of the tables at the back wall. They went through it and up some stairs that seemed to lead outside. They went through a door and found themselves on the roof.

Janna gasped at the sight in front of her. A helicopter was waiting, blades whirring, and she realized she must have been really intent on her work not to hear it approach. Ryder's thick, dark hair whipped in the wind and he reached out a hand. She took it, and his strong grip guided her up into the cabin. She belted up, still agape, and he sat across from her, grinning like a cat that had gotten into the cream.

"Good surprise," she said, bracing herself against the wall as it started to take off.

"I'm glad," he said. He leaned back like he'd done this a hundred times, and maybe he had, and eyed her with that gleam that made her squirm in her seat.

He looked at her like she was the only woman in the world, and she didn't know what to do with that fact.

"Where are you taking me?" she asked over the whir of the motor.

"You'll see." His face was calm as he leaned forward to speak to the pilot. He was commanding, serious, until he turned back to her with that panty-melting smile. She squirmed again, gripping the seat next to her. Heaven forbid they end up alone in the cabin again. She didn't know what she would do.

She closed her eyes and took a deep breath, then looked out over the mountain as they flew up along the ridge. Breathtaking. He reached out a hand for hers and she took it and let it rest on her knee. A guy who took her in a helicopter could have that and more. She blushed at the thought and kept her eyes on the scenery. Otherwise, she'd be tempted to rake his body again, look at his chest, his tight waist, powerful shoulders, and um, below the belt. She swallowed nervously and forced herself to stay facing the window.

SHE WAS ADORABLE. RYDER COULDN'T hide his smile at her excitement, so he was glad she was turned to the window, rather than watching him beam at her creepily. He couldn't help it. Already, her happiness was his happiness. If he'd met her before, he had no doubt they'd have settled into exactly this already. What if he'd never left town?

No, then he wouldn't be Ryder Hart, the man he was now. And maybe she wouldn't even want him. That thought rankled. Would she have wanted him as just the heir to a minor tourist hotel? He frowned but pushed away any darkness by watching her gaze eagerly out at the scenery flying by. He'd been up here before, so it wasn't anything new to him. But it was new taking someone special. It was definitely new being here with a beautiful woman.

He had lunch planned in the little mountain lodge that had been his father's private retreat. *And probably where he brought his women*, he thought with a frown.

But that wouldn't ruin his day with Janna. When the chopper landed, he helped her out, and the pilot took off, presumably for a day of heli-skiing with someone like Ryan. Ryder had his own ideas for getting down the mountain.

He carried the basket he'd had the chef put together. Nothing fancy, just some sandwiches, chips, and dessert, but anything would be fun with Janna. She followed him curiously to the lodge door and he opened it for her to go inside first, enjoying the sway of her hips as she went. Damn, he just wanted to pick her up and take her to his bedroom and make love to her again.

But first things first. Wooing.

He could be a gentleman even if he was half bear.

She sat at the rustic table and let out an exclamation of pleasure when he pulled out the food. "Ryder, this is too much."

He scratched his head and grinned. "I told you…"

"You like 'em well fed. I get it. I get it." But she didn't seem mad about it, and she talked about the reports while they ate together. There was an easy kind of mood between them, apart from the sizzling sexual tension that felt like it was ready to break at any moment. But Ryder wasn't going to lose control a second time. Not if it was going to give his future mate the wrong idea.

But she kept looking up at him from under her eyelashes with furtive glances, deep-brown eyes flashing with some unknown emotion, and darned if it didn't keep making his pants tight in the most uncomfortable way. And there was no way to shift position while being a gentleman. So he sat there in near agony, trying to focus on what she was saying and not on the velvety lips speaking the words.

Damn.

When lunch finished and she sat back with a sigh of contentment, Ryder felt ready to burst. He stood hurriedly and tugged on his jacket. "Ready to go?" He couldn't wait to show her the next surprise and get outside where the cold air could cool his ardor. She wasn't his yet. He had to go slow.

He put out an arm, loving the feel of her small, gloved hand on his forearm, and led her around the side of the cabin, which was shielded from the cold. His own personal snowmobile was waiting for him, and Janna let out another squeak of pleasure when she saw it.

"You ever ridden one of these?" he asked.

She shook her head. "No, but I'm game. Except you aren't going to try and get me in ski lessons next, are you?"

"Why?" he asked, straddling the seat and reaching for her. "Too much for the Cali girl to handle?"

She smirked and got on behind him. "Never. But a girl can only take so much excitement in one week."

"Baby," he said, feeling cheesy but unable to stop himself, "whatever you can take, I'm going to give you."

She laughed, and he felt it vibrate through him as she pressed against him and wrapped her arms around his middle. Her soft breasts pressed into his back and he groaned. She made him feel like a teenager again. His dad should have warned him that finding your mate made your hormones act like they'd never seen a woman before.

He was Ryder Hart. Billionaire. Magnate. Always in control.

Except with this curvaceous, playful woman who seemed to always be one step ahead. Even when they'd made love, she'd been with him every step of the way, leading and wanting and moaning her pleasure until he did what she wanted.

Damn did he want to do that again.

He hadn't been lying when he told her what Ryder Hart wants, Ryder Hart gets.

But that didn't mean the acquisition would be an easy one. Then again, he usually found the more difficult an asset was to acquire, the more worth having it was.

He started up the snowmobile and, after making sure Janna was holding on tight, started down the mountain.

The snow was falling lightly, packed in tight drifts on the trees around them and slowly fluttering to ground when disturbed by the wind. Despite the sound of the motor and the whoosh of the air going past, there was something so still and quiet about the white all around them.

His heart was warm, knowing it was just them here alone together. There wouldn't be skiers or snowboarders on this hill. It was private and marked off with signs that warned against trespassing.

There were apparently some benefits to being a lodge owner and having your own mountain. Even in this little tourist town mostly known for skiing and bears.

The bears around here should be hibernating, but sometimes they were disturbed. And then there were bear shifters who didn't follow those rules. Even bear shifters that could shift had varying levels of bear blood. Having any bear was just so rare compared to the other shifter races.

He wondered how he'd explain that to Janna.

He could almost feel her heartbeat against his back; he was that close to her. He could smell her arousal at their touch, remember the scent from last night, and he found himself hitting the gas too hard in response. He told himself to go slower, but they still found themselves back at the base of the lodge all too soon, to both their chagrin.

She seemed reluctant to get off and get back to work. When she got off the snowmobile and made as if she were leaving, he caught her by the hand and pulled her back, catching her lips with his.

The kiss was gentle, the antithesis of the other night, and when he pulled back, a single snowflake fell on her bottom lip, melting when he came back against her. He loved the fit they had, the feel of her, and he pulled her body against him as he gently deepened the kiss. When he let her go, she stumbled slightly and he put a hand out to steady her.

"Full of surprises," she murmured, touching her lips. Her hair was in beautiful disarray from the ride, extra curly and wild. He wanted to see how it would look fresh out of bed.

"Thanks," he said. "I had a great time."

"So," she said, composing herself and smoothing down her coat. "Back to work?"

He sighed and got off the snowmobile to follow her in. "I suppose." He put an arm around her and was rewarded with a grin. "If we have to."

She nodded and led the way into the lodge. "Work before play."

Ryder sort of wished it were the other way around.

CHAPTER
TEN

THE REST OF THE WORKDAY went by briskly, except for a couple of interruptions from Ryder's brothers to tease them about working on vacation.

But Ryder was difficult to ruffle, so she hid her blush and worked alongside him and tried not to react to the teasing. What was really on her mind was what was going to happen once they were at the cabin again. And the fact that she shouldn't ever ride on a snowmobile behind Ryder again. It was far too dangerous. The feel of his wide back against her soft breasts, the hard abs under her hands. It had been heaven.

She made a note to call her girlfriends for some girl time the next day. It was exactly what she needed to clear her head. That thought reminded her of the phone message, and she drummed her fingers on the desk while thinking whether she should tell Ryder.

She would wait and see if more messages came. She knew she was safe here, and perhaps if she showed him, he'd overreact. She'd just have to be cautious.

He was putting away papers briskly and eyeing the clock, and she put away what she was working on as well. They'd made good progress, often with long stretches of silence, which suited her well because she preferred that when trying to focus.

But now that work was wrapping up, all she could feel was the tension in the air around them.

In a few minutes, he'd be taking her back to the cabin. And she didn't know if she could handle that.

At the end of this week, she could very well be going back to her small apartment and her small business and the daily visits from her ex and the weekly girls' nights out.

That hadn't been too bad, up until Ryder Hart walked into her life. Deciding she needed a dose of reality, she pulled out her phone and fidgeted with it until Ryder looked over at her, puzzled.

"You need to call someone?" he asked, drawing up to full height to look down at her. Damn he was tall.

"I was thinking about calling the girls." Disappointment flashed across his face but was gone quickly, and he smiled politely.

"Sure. If you'd like, I'll send the jeep for them. I don't want you to feel lonely up here while you're working."

She got the impression that he'd like to be the one keeping her from being lonely, but she appreciated that he didn't have any problem with girl time. If what they had gone longer than this week? He'd need to be okay with her girlfriends. That was non-negotiable. "That would be great, thanks."

An unreadable expression moved over his features and he nodded and ducked out to make a phone call. She dialed on hers as well.

Leslie was first to pick up.

"Hello? Where the hell have you been?" she asked, sounding exasperated and relieved at the same time. "You weren't at work, and Sherry said something about going off for a week with some guy, and I *know* you weren't planning to not tell your best friends about it!"

Janna laughed, wincing a little at Leslie's exuberance. She couldn't help but think she'd be a good match with Riley. Both seemed to have a little too much energy at times and too much fun interfering in other people's lives. But she loved Leslie all the same.

"It's Ryder."

"Ryder Hart? Um, excuse me, but if you're on a first-name basis with Ryder Hart, then I need details immediately. Not that I'm not supportive of you finally stepping out of Scott's shadow, but come on, girl. Deets!"

"Give me a second to talk," Janna said. "Ryder was thinking of sending down a Jeep to pick you and Kylie up to bring you to the lodge. I'm staying here right now."

Leslie let out a wolf whistle. "Wow, when you step out of that prissy shell, you really—"

"We're working on paperwork together. His father's accountant really made a mess of things, and Ryder hired me for a week to sort it out with him."

"Mm-hmm." Leslie didn't sound convinced. Janna knew she was probably right. But still, she had to try the less controversial story first. "As for the Jeep, sure, that'd be fun. Kylie was coming over tonight and we were going to make plans to stalk you, so I guess this works."

"Stalk me, hm?" Janna teased. "Or were you simply hoping the mysterious man I was with was one of the brothers and you'd be able to chill with them too?"

"Pssh. Like you'd hold out on us. There's three of them. Three. You've got the billionaire. Share the wealth."

"I haven't got anything. And you're welcome to any of the men." She fidgeted nervously as she said it. She wasn't really sure that was true. If anyone else showed interest in Ryder…

"Sure, sure. I can tell from your voice something is up," Leslie said. That was probably true. Leslie was uncannily good at reading people. Maybe it had something to do with being a bartender.

"Well, maybe," she said, thinking of what had happened when they got to the cabin the other night. She felt hot from head to toe, and Leslie made a hissing noise.

"You screwed him, didn't you? Janna, you naughty accountant!"

"Hey, accountants gotta have fun, too. After all, we don't have exciting careers like you."

"Ha! Listening to sad drunks and fending off tourist advances? Not that exciting."

"So come up here and get you some excitement," Janna said. "Bring Kylie. I totally need girl time."

"Girl, if I had the chance to get any of those men alone, girl time is the last thing I would want."

"Hm," Janna replied.

"Trust," Leslie said. "I'm just warning you. If I get an opening, I'm moving in. You don't get men like that out here often. I mean, damn."

Damn indeed. Janna couldn't argue with the sentiment, given that just yesterday she'd thrown her cares to the wind and just gone with it.

"So… how was it?" Leslie asked after a pause. Janna could hear the smile in her voice.

"Hm, I don't kiss and tell."

"Yes, you damn well do! We all do! Now spill."

"I can't," Janna said, twirling a piece of hair around her finger, kind of pleased to be the one with actual adventure to share. "He's just outside."

"Well, say it in code or something."

"Code?"

"Something he won't know what you're saying," Leslie spat out.

"Hm. Well, let's just say he's a *big* deal," Janna said, trying to keep from laughing. "And he's *good* at his job. And he's a great… *multitasker.*"

"Girrrl…" Leslie muttered. "I'mma need more deets when I get there." A knock sounded in the background. "That's Kylie. I'm going to go tell her. When will the Jeep be here?"

"As soon as Ryder can send them. Do you want me to come down?"

"Nah, you can just be ready to greet us with a big entrance. And, Janna?"

"Yes?"

"Try and get the other boys there."

She sighed. She supposed it wasn't fair to hold out on them. They'd had so many girls' nights dreaming and talking of men like this, and now she had an in. She'd just have to hope Ryder wouldn't take it wrong. "All right, I'll try."

"You're the best."

"No, you are," she told Leslie. Truly feeling like she didn't know how she would have survived without the other woman. Leslie simply chuckled, blew a kiss into the phone, and hung up.

When Janna exited the office, Ryder was waiting.

"You get a hold of your friends?" he asked.

"Yes, they're up for it."

"Great, give me the address and I'll send the Jeep. The driver's already waiting outside."

"Perfect," she said, writing it down for him. He ran it outside and she enjoyed the look of his taut ass and long legs. Who knew smart guys could be so hot? She liked being with him, partly because he always seemed to have things under control. Always had a plan or was ready to come up with one. Always thinking one step ahead. It was such a relief after a man-child like Scott, who'd expected her to handle most things herself and whined when he didn't get his way.

Watching Ryder walk back to her, swishing dark hair off his forehead and smiling, she felt her heart skip a beat, and for the first time, was almost a little glad that Scott had cheated on her.

Without him, she wouldn't be here.

Or would she? A silly, romantic part of her felt maybe she and Ryder would have met otherwise.

She shook her head, stunned by her thoughts. Though she'd been smitten by Scott, she'd never had any thoughts about fate or destiny with him.

Was it simply that Ryder was a billionaire, rich and handsome, that was sweeping her off her feet? No, there had to be more. It was like the air was electric when their eyes met. His touch was unbelievably hot yet perfectly suited to her.

She was glad they wouldn't be alone tonight. She didn't know if she'd be able to keep her hands off his hard, muscled body. Not after everything he'd done for her today. And all of the sweet conversation they'd had.

No, company would be perfect.

She didn't trust herself around Ryder Hart. She was too likely to make a fool of herself over him. He was everything she'd want in a man, if she could order it. Integrity, openness, control, protectiveness. She could easily fall in love with him.

"You okay? What do you think they'd like to eat for dinner?" he asked as he approached.

She fidgeted and then dropped her phone in her pocket. "I don't know. Steak never goes wrong."

"I was thinking more party food. What do you think about pizza? Fancy pizza, of course, because that's what they have here. And drinks. And snacks."

"That sounds great," she said. "And can you invite your brothers?"

"Sure," he said. "No problem." He turned as if he were going to go call them and then stopped, hesitating. He gave her a slightly dark look, and she realized with astonishment that he was jealous of her asking for them to be there.

"No, no," she said, waving her hands in front of her in a placating gesture. "Leslie and Kylie wanted them to be here."

Relief washed over his handsome features and an adorable dimple appeared in his cheek. "That's fine. I'm sure they don't need any inducement to hang out with a couple of beautiful women."

It was Janna's turn to feel jealous, and she didn't like Ryder calling her friends beautiful, even if they were.

"Don't get me wrong," he said. "Not as beautiful as you."

She flushed and then laughed at being caught in the same position as him. "It's all right. Is it okay if I freshen up before dinner?" she asked.

"Sure," he said. "Just stay close."

"I was just going to go to the cabin. You gave me a set of keys, after all. And my stuff is there."

His face tensed and a corner of his mouth turned down. "I'll walk you over."

"There's no need…"

He seemed to sense that she wanted to go on her own, so he shrugged and followed her to the entrance closest to the path that led to the cabin. "All right, I'll watch you from here."

She prickled. "I'm really fine."

"What about the bears?" he asked, and there seemed to be a hidden meaning there.

"Oh. I thought they'd be gone."

"I'll watch from here," he said.

She looked at the stubborn tilt of his jaw and realized she wasn't going to get her way with him, so she just stood on tiptoe to place a kiss gently on his jaw, which was lightly roughened with stubble. She breathed in his uniquely masculine scent and then stepped away. She didn't miss the subtle, sharp intake of breath he'd made when she kissed him or the fire burning in his eyes as he watched her walk away.

She could see him in the glass behind her, watching her with eyes that were sharp and wanting.

Wanting something she wanted right back.

She stepped out into the cold, grateful for the evening air to cool her mind. A week with Ryder Hart? She was never going to make it that long without making a fool of herself or breaking her heart.

But she was going to try. She'd risked more for less. She grinned as she entered her cabin to get ready for the night.

CHAPTER
ELEVEN

RYDER GULPED IN AIR, TRYING to get adequate breath as Janna walked into the lodge with her friends.

The three women all looked very different. Kylie was the shortest, with straight blond hair and a shy, pretty face with round eyes and small features. Leslie had big wavy curls in her dark hair, and her skin was a lighter brown than Janna's. Her eyes, however, were black.

And then there was his future mate. She'd gelled her curls so they made tight little ringlets all over her head. Her full lips were glossed in deep pink, and her warm-brown eyes sparkled at him with amusement. And that was just above the neck. Should he dare to look below…

She was wearing a little black dress tonight. Sleeveless, under a coat. It draped over her magnificent breasts and hugged her soft hourglass waist with a belted tie before falling softly over those hips that he just wanted to take hold of and grab as he sucked her off.

Her curvy brown legs showed some deep, rich skin before disappearing into stylish black booties that covered her delicate feet up to the heel.

Damn. He just wanted to run over, shield her from everyone else's view, pick her up, and run to the cabin. See those dark curls spread over his pillow, those full lips parted in pleasure.

She turned to laugh at something one of her friends said and the sound was magical. His heart tightened. The warmth around her was familiar somehow. He thought maybe it reminded him somewhat of his mother. How he and his brothers had loved that sound.

It had been a long time since he'd dared to love a woman like that. Allowed himself to love one so much that even her laugh felt like something to chase after, if only to hear it again and again.

If his mother could see him now, would she be proud of his choice in Janna? How he was treating her? She'd had a whirlwind romance of her own, and he wished she were around to ask how to go about it.

But there was something warm and feminine in his life again. And this time, she would be his mate. He would take care of her. His to protect, and he would.

He felt the stares of other men in the lodge, their hungry eyes raking the women from head to toe. Settling especially on Janna, who seemed to be more and more full of life the more time they spent together.

Damn, she was a light attracting moths. He wanted to hide her in his bedroom, but that was no way to treat a lady.

At least Ryder Hart knew that. Ryder Hart's bear was still voting for a trip to the cave.

He walked forward, confident in the nice suit he'd picked for dinner, standing tall and letting the other men know who was alpha here. He reached out an arm for Janna to take, and the other women tittered in response. Janna blushed but put her hand softly on his bicep, and he fought the tightening feeling that always happened when she touched him.

Something told him they'd be back at the cabin tonight, making another "mistake."

Janna introduced her friends as they walked. Kylie was the town florist and occasionally substitute taught at the local school. Leslie owned a bar in town and also was the go-to person for events. She was vivacious and sparkly and he couldn't help being reminded of Riley.

He wasn't sure these two should be in the same room together.

They asked him questions about business, what he was doing in town, and how his brothers were doing as they walked to the restaurant together. He'd rented out the private conference room for their little group date.

His brothers had grumbled. Not because they didn't want to meet the women, but because Ryder had threatened them with death if they did anything ungentlemanly and upset the friends of his mate. They had agreed to be docile, but he knew that still meant no promises. They were bears. Alphas at that. The top of the shifter food chain and world famous to boot— Riley for his acting, Ryan for his snowboarding.

Kylie asked the most questions about Ryan. Ryder couldn't answer a lot of them, mainly because Ryan was a fairly aloof, distant person, preferring to spend his time with the mountains and the outdoors. He'd taken to hanging out with the ski and snowboard instructor crew and had been testing the new park and complaining about the height of the rollers.

Ryder had tried to point out that most tourists weren't trying to pull off inverted rotations, but Ryan hadn't been swayed.

Ryan probably would end up building more on the park for his own purpose. Hopefully, no one would end up getting killed on it.

Riley and Ryan were waiting for them inside the room. The table was a little odd. It was sunken into the ground, a large, square hole surrounding it, and everyone was expected to sit on cushions on the edge that surrounded the table, their legs in front of them between the bench edge and the table. But it made for an intimate feeling between guests.

Riley was wearing a purple button-up that set off his lightly tanned skin and blondish-brown hair perfectly. He flashed his movie-star smile at the women, and Kylie froze. Leslie, however, walked right in. Riley's hazel eyes widened slightly when Leslie sat directly across from him, but his easy smile came right back and Ryder doubted anyone but he or Ryan would have caught Riley's momentary lack of ease.

Kylie surprised him by walking over and sitting next to Ryan, who was sitting in a tee shirt with one of his sponsor's logos on it. Ryan never seemed to feel cold. The restaurant was properly heated, but at the same time, this wasn't California.

Ryan's toned arms extended out of his shirt, and he leaned back with a look of consternation as the little blonde plopped herself down right next to him. His panicked eyes flew to Ryder, and Ryder just shrugged. He wasn't any better with women than Ryan was.

Ryan let Kylie introduce herself but kept his distance, eyeing her like he thought he might break her.

They were all big boys, at 6'7" or so, but they didn't usually notice it when they were all together. But throw women into the equation, even tall ones like Leslie and Janna, and suddenly they felt like giants trying not to trample everything in their paths.

Throw in a little thing like Kylie, and it was enough to make any bear nervous.

But Janna was smooth and quick to make introductions. She sat next to him, thigh pressing against his and making his groin tighten painfully. Damn, the softness of that skin. Nothing was like that in the world.

Riley was on his other side, grinning knowingly. But Ryder doubted he knew his thoughts. His brothers knew him as a stiff, unrelenting person who always got his own way. They'd never know he was holding himself back, trying to win this woman even if it meant letting her take the reins.

On the other side of the table, Leslie was across from Riley, Kylie was next to her, and Ryan was on the other side, across from Janna. And checking her out.

Ryder stifled a low growl and gave his brother a hearty, quiet kick under the table. Ryan grunted and shifted his gaze, giving Ryder a nod of apology. It wasn't his fault Janna was so beautiful, but Ryder meant to see that no one disrespected her while he was around.

And okay, a lot of it was jealousy too. He already saw her as his. He didn't like anyone else looking. He tilted his head sideways to look at her and caught a full view of cleavage as she looked over her menu. How he wanted to caress the dark velvet of her skin. Taste her where he hadn't yet gotten a chance to. Run his fingers over the tops of her plump breasts.

Then he realized someone had asked him a question. Damn!

"I said, do you do much skiing?" Leslie asked, resting her chin on her hand smugly, probably for having caught him staring at Janna like a man out of control.

"Not really," he said. "I mean, for conferences or meet-ups sometimes, yes. In my free time, I prefer more..." He glanced at Janna. "Relaxing endeavors."

Leslie's grin widened and Janna blushed and discussed the menu with Kylie.

He wanted to keep Janna on her toes. Remind her he was here, even if they were in a room full of people. For him, there was only her. And he was a little jealous she could pay so much attention to the others. He knew it was a little childish, but then he was used to getting his way. And bears were known for being selfish creatures.

Out in the wild, they were basically the assholes of the woods. Mating promiscuously and leaving after. But when a bear spirit was mixed with a human one, there could be a tempering. The strength and fortitude of the bear that made him and his brothers so successful. But the goodness and integrity of what a man can choose to be. Good to women. Faithful to one mate. Happy that way.

He believed it could be that way at least.

Leslie went back to badgering Riley about fame, about how he was discovered, even though that was common knowledge and she already had to know. Everyone did. He'd been scouted in college at a party, and the rest had been history.

He always played the action hero or romantic interest. Just his abs were enough to get women filling the seats. Which was good, because the writing for some of the Riley Hart movies was downright embarrassing.

He noted with amusement that Kylie kept trying to squeeze over toward Ryan, and Ryan was practically ready to pull his legs out and scoot away from the table.

He put his hand over Janna's, warm and secure, letting her know he was there. She turned to him with a smile, and heat shot right down to his toes.

The need to claim her was strong. He swore he could literally hear the roar of his bear waiting to claim her. She squeezed his hand back, and he released hers and moved his hand to her thigh. So soft.

She bit her bottom lip and made a tiny gasp that had the others looking her way.

"Sorry," she said apologetically. "Bit my lip while looking at the menu. It all looks so good."

The men grinned at her. Whether it was because they knew what Ryder's hand had been up to or because they liked that she liked the food, Ryder didn't know. But he let out a low growl and shut the menus either way. He opened the sliding door, called for a waiter, and just ordered a ton of things that should probably suit everyone. He'd order the whole menu if he had to. Just to hurry this along and keep his brothers' eyes off his mate.

And to be able to take her back home.

For dessert.

He caught Riley raking the other two women with an appreciative gaze. Even Ryan, when he wasn't eyeing Kylie with a wary stare, was checking out the females. The women were all pleasantly curvy and soft. Exactly what bears tended to go for. All shifters really. Not that lean couldn't be attractive, but the softer and larger, the better for bears. Kylie was even on the small side, despite being what others might consider overweight.

Leslie took most of the attention, and that seemed to suit Kylie.

Ryder kept his eyes primarily on Janna, both to make sure she knew he had eyes only for her and because he *liked* keeping his eyes on Janna.

By the end of the night, maybe he'd have more than just eyes on her.

A knock sounded on the door and the waiter entered. Followed by another waiter. All in all, it took three waiters to deliver the amount of food he'd ordered, and Janna raised an eyebrow at him when it was all covering the table.

He shrugged innocently but was secretly pleased there was plenty to go around. His brothers could eat a lot, not that they would before the women had their fill. Females were more important.

He poured a glass of wine for himself and Janna and offered it around the table. Riley took it and filled Leslie's and Kylie's glass, and Ryan waved it away. Bad for training, he said.

The Olympics aren't for another three years, Riley had reminded him, but Ryan had declined all the same.

Once an athlete, always an athlete.

When the dinner finished, Janna was fidgeting in her seat. The other women were standing and saying good night, hugging her from behind as she reluctantly stood, and she merely smiled slightly in return. Was she sad to see them go? No, he couldn't call it sad exactly. Was she worried without them he'd make a move? Nervous? He'd make sure to try and assuage that. He wanted his mate, but he'd never do anything to make her uncomfortable.

He and Janna linked arms and Ryan and Riley walked with them to escort the women back out to the Jeep. Kylie had said she was teaching the next day and would need to be up early, and Leslie seemed disappointed that Riley wasn't making a move.

Ryder was sure Riley would have, if not for Ryder's threatening glares throughout the night. He could make whatever moves he wanted after Ryder was assured Janna would be his mate. After that, it was Leslie and Riley's business. But he didn't need drama screwing things up now. Janna was already gun shy from being burned by Scott. She didn't need an angry friend helping her make the decision.

And Leslie would probably be angry because Riley had a strictly love 'em and leave 'em kind of style. He'd make sure to tell Janna so she could warn her friend. At least then she'd know what she was getting into.

He didn't want to see anyone hurt.

When the women had given hugs to all and left, he found himself standing with his brothers and Janna. It was awkward. He cleared his throat.

"I guess I'm going to get Janna settled in for the night."

"Right," Riley joked. "Settled in."

Ryder let out a low growl and rose to full height to face his brother. Riley put up his hands in surrender. "All right, all right. We can take a hint. We know when we aren't wanted. Come on, Ryan, let's go drink our woes away at the lodge bar."

Ryan nodded but paused to put a hand on Ryder's shoulder as he passed.

Ryder looked to him, waiting for what he wanted to say. Janna was still looking out to where the Jeep was pulling away, and when Ryan seemed assured she wasn't listening, he leaned in to whisper in Ryder's ear.

"She's a good one," he said quietly. "I like her."

Ryder blinked. That was high praise from Ryan, a quiet, sensitive type who tended not to give opinions very often. "Thanks, bro."

Ryan nodded and jogged after Riley, who was already prowling toward the bar, probably looking for any single ladies on the way.

He took a step forward and put an arm around Janna's waist, pulling her against him. She turned in his arms and looked up at him. Damn, she seemed small compared to him. Small and precious.

But she was a woman. Capable, smart, and strong. If she chose him, it would only be because she wanted to.

"We don't have to do anything tonight," he said. "I don't want you to feel pressured."

Her eyes blinked up at him and her jaw tilted stubbornly. "What makes you think I feel pressured?"

"You seemed nervous that your friends were leaving. But if you were worried I'd suddenly come on to you, you shouldn't have."

"Ha!" she said, putting her hands on his chest, warming the skin there. "I was hoping you'd come on to me."

His groin tightened at that and he bit his lip against a groan.

"Honestly," she said. "The only thing worrying me is how little control I seem to have around you. My rational mind just flies out the window. I want you so badly I can barely walk."

He tilted his head and looked down at her, and a slow smile curled the corners of his lips. "I can carry you."

She reached her arms up toward him. "Yes, please."

He grinned and swept her up in his arms, not caring who saw as he carried his mate bridal style out of the lodge and to the cabin they shared.

It was going to be a good night.

CHAPTER
TWELVE

THEY WERE ALREADY PULLING AT each other's clothes as they fell in the cabin door together after Ryder set Janna down. She pulled at his suit coat, which was tight across his wide shoulders.

He looked so freaking good in that suit, but she had a feeling he'd look better without it. His dark hair was combed back and swept off his forehead, and his handsome features were tensed and focused as he reached around her with a growl and unzipped her dress.

She laughed. "Take off my coat first!"

He growled. Literally growled. "I have to taste you."

She dropped her arms and let her coat slide to the floor and then grabbed at his coat again until he mumbled a curse and shrugged out of it for her.

His tailored white dress shirt was taut across his chest and he fumbled with the buttons as his mouth claimed hers.

Her dress was barely hanging on, and when he finished unbuttoning his shirt and shrugged out of it, leaving him only in an undershirt, he swept his hands over her shoulders and down her waist, smoothing the dress off her body until it let go and pooled on the ground in a puddle of black silk.

She growled and reached up on her toes, trying to wrap her arms around his neck, and he caught her up and lifted her so she could wrap her legs around his waist. Damn, she felt tall up here, perched above his long legs, her soft thighs enjoying the taut feel of his rippling abs. He held her up with one strong hand and pulled off his undershirt with the other, leaving her warm belly pressed to his searing hot skin. He felt literally on fire, but in a good way.

His hand cupped her ass, thumb playing with the waistband of her panties, and she sighed as his other hand moved to hold her back so he could lean forward and press a kiss to the side of her neck. She gasped as he nipped the skin there and turned around and walked her back into the door they'd just entered through. There were no open windows in the cabin. They'd shut them all before leaving so they didn't have to worry about anyone seeing them.

It was just them alone, a man and a woman ensconced together with wilderness all around, the snowy mountains a distant witness to their lovemaking.

He loved her tenderly, with his mouth, his hands, warming her and getting her ready by treasuring each inch of her skin he could reach. Feeling, caressing, stroking, pinching, laving.

He got her bra off and raised her up so he could take her nipple in his mouth. As he tasted it and she threw her head back in ecstasy, he seemed to lose all control. He walked quickly forward to drop her on the couch, then looked it over as if it weren't good enough and picked her back up in his arms and carried her against his chest into the bedroom.

A little thrill went through her. They'd have a full time together tonight, not a rushed interlude on the couch.

The mattress was soft and large, and he settled her on it gently but then crawled over her with a growl, his large body covering hers as he nearly purred with satisfaction.

If this was the kind of passion Ryder Hart used to acquire companies, then she could understand why he was a billionaire.

He kissed her neck as he slid her panties off her legs. He lifted his head and his sapphire eyes darkened to nearly onyx as he breathed in the air in the room.

"You smell amazing."

She swatted him with her hand. "Ew, don't talk about it."

He dipped his head between her legs and inhaled again, let out a hoarse oath, and came forward to claim her mouth with a potent strength unlike any she'd ever experienced. When he was done ravaging her mouth and she was gasping for air and imagining wickeder things he could do to her, he lifted his head and smiled that cocky smile that made her knees go weak.

He wasn't a man to smile often, but when he did, it was a knockout.

"I'll talk about it if I want," he said. "I love everything about you." He drew his lips down the center of her chest, kissing the inside curves of her breasts as he gathered them gently in his large hands. It felt so good to be held by a man. If someone could invent a bra that cupped her like this, she'd buy ten of them.

A week.

Her breasts felt treasured. Every part of her felt awake and alive as his touch moved over her. He seemed determined to trace his ownership on every inch of skin, grazing her ankle and toes, kissing her inner thigh and turning her over to do the same with her back. When he sat back on his knees and lifted her hand to press a kiss to the tips of her fingers, she squirmed in anticipation. Her whole body felt more sensitive the longer he continued. The foreplay was torture.

When he sucked one of her fingers into his hot mouth, as no one had ever done before, she was shocked by the powerful pleasure that rocked through her.

The sight of that huge, strong man gazing at her with lust as she relinquished her hand and came forward over her tortured body nearly did her in, but he pressed his mouth over hers and slowed things down as he gently stroked with his tongue and wrapped his arms around her.

He moved and whispered against her ear in a way that tickled. "Can I taste you everywhere?"

"I think you have," she gasped out, unable to keep from smiling.

"Not everywhere," he replied in a husky voice, drawing one finger over the soft thatch at the top of her thighs.

"Oh," she gasped. "That. Um, sure."

It was something she'd never let Scott do, something she'd been too embarrassed to ask for, though he'd demanded blowjobs. She got the sense he was slightly grossed out by the idea. But Ryder seemed positively hungry, and she longed to be appreciated that way. To feel that no part of her was dirty as woman. To be loved even where she was most insecure.

His hands kneaded her belly gently as he moved down the bed. "Relax," he said, smoothing a hand over her soft middle before using his other to part her legs in one smooth motion.

He was so strong. She knew he could do whatever he wanted whenever he wanted, but he'd asked. He'd been gentle and concerned about her feelings.

Ryder Hart was definitely too good to be true. And she was no fool. But even if this ended up breaking her heart, it was worth it. A memory to keep for forever.

She'd never forget him.

As he lowered his mouth and kissed her center gently, she felt her muscles tense up further, desperate for release. She reached down and dug her hands in his hair. She was already so close from everything else he'd done. Everything he did had an impact on her.

"Harder," she gasped.

He sucked down right over her center and then swirled his tongue in a slow circle around and over it, and she screamed and arched back in the most intense orgasm she'd ever had.

But he didn't let go, licking and sucking and kissing as she writhed against him and was sent into another rhythmic orgasm, her body contracting all over as waves of pleasure and relief roared from head to toe. Even the fingers where he'd kissed her. Every inch of her body, like he'd been setting it up that way just by paying that kind of attention to her.

She let go of his hair and twisted her fingers in the sheets, but he was relentless, moving against her with his strong tongue until the build started again, and then rushed her over the edge of another orgasm and into a rush of oblivion followed by seconds of sheer, screaming pleasure.

She screamed his name, not caring who heard, and she could swear she felt him grin against her pussy.

When he finally raised his head to gaze down at her as she lay there, exhausted from coming but not even close to satisfied, the pleasure he'd gained from pleasing her was evident on his face. When he made to lower his head again, she sat up slightly with a growl and shook her head. She grabbed his face in both hands, kissed him hard, and then growled into his ear.

"Take me now."

A deep rumble in his throat was his assent, and he pressed her back with one hand and pulled off pants and boxer briefs in one smooth movement. His manhood sprang free, and he reached for a condom, ripped the packet open, and slid it on.

Then his hands were on either side of her head, his eyes gazing into hers, glowing with sapphire intensity, and then he was inside her, stretching her, pushing her body to the edge of its limits of pleasure. Making the sensitive place inside her light up like it was on fire, the best kind of fire that heats but doesn't burn. She let her body adjust and took a couple deep breaths and then wrapped her legs around his waist, locking her legs at the heels. She wasn't letting him out.

He closed his eyes as he started to move. She felt her body moving with him, staying joined and then pulling a little apart, so that delicious friction that resulted from each ridge of him stimulated every space inside her.

She'd never felt so filled, so complete, and at some point during the heights of the ecstasy between them, she looked up into his eyes and realized she no longer knew where he ended and she began.

It was a cosmic feeling, the best in the world, and also a little frightening. She wrapped her hands around him as her orgasm came, and he held her tight with one hand and thrust a few more times until he found his own completion. He uttered a low oath and then her name and then something she couldn't quite make out.

She dug her nails in as her orgasm resonated against his where they were joined and held him as they rode the waves together.

When it abated, she dropped back against the pillows and he fell over her. She ran a finger through a lock that had come free, and he sighed hoarsely.

"Would it be crazy to say I love you?" he asked.

"Yes," she said, knowing she could feel similarly if she let herself, but wouldn't.

"I don't care, I'll say it anyway. I love you, Janna. Spend your life with me."

She froze, pleasure still waving over her, his body still pleasantly ensconced in hers, and his warm strength covering her like he wanted to protect her from everything in the world.

"I'll make sure you're always happy," he said. "I'll never let anything happen to you."

She stroked his hair, loving the dark softness of it. He had so much. So much of everything to offer really. So why couldn't her heart get on board and trust him?

Stupid Scott.

"You don't have to say that," she said. "I know that's not what this is."

He flinched and lifted himself, narrowing his eyes at her as his jaw tightened. "What?"

She waved a hand weakly. "I just mean I'm already going to stay with you this week. You don't need to make this out like it's more than it is. I prefer honesty, and it's not like I wouldn't stay with you anyway."

His expression darkened and he pulled gently out and caught himself with a towel. Then he rolled to the side of the bed to clean up.

She couldn't help but feel tenderness as she stared at the sight of his large, wide back, the hunch of his shoulders as he worked.

"What kind of man do you think I am, Janna?" he asked, giving her a dark expression as he crossed to the closet and flung open the doors. He pulled out a pair of soft-looking pajama pants in navy blue and pulled them on with hasty motions. "You think I'd use you like that?"

She shrugged, hating this had to happen while she was still enjoying her afterglow. "We're both adults. We're having fun together, right? I mean, I know men feel like they have to say I love you every time, but let's be honest. You barely know me."

He flinched like she'd struck him, and she couldn't tell why he'd be hurt by that. It was true. Any woman would probably think twice about believing a man loved her and wanted to spend his life with her after only two days.

What made him so different that it should be believable?

"What if I told you I knew, deep down in a special part of myself, that I'm meant for you and you're meant for me?" he asked, still facing away.

He was striking too close to home, to those romantic fantasies she'd once had of meeting the one and living happily ever after with a prince. And she'd been hurt too much before by believing them. He couldn't expect her to do that now. Not yet.

"I'd say you were crazy," she said. "And maybe just getting a bit caught up."

He growled and strode toward the bed. His magnificent bare chest caught the lamplight as he lunged onto the bed and took her mouth in another fierce kiss. This one was claiming, harsh, a sign of ownership, and when he pulled back, she found herself once again unable to think rationally.

And that scared her.

"I'm not crazy," he said. "I don't just say this to women. I don't use women who I know are looking for something long term. I knew when I looked at you, just by how Scott had hurt you, that you're the type a man keeps forever. I'm looking for forever, Janna."

She turned away on a sob. "I don't know if I can believe in forever anymore," she said. "And it's just too good to be true. You don't know how it felt. To move out here to the middle of nowhere, to the wilderness, because I thought I was going to be loved, protected. Instead, I wound up alone. Poor. Nowhere to go. Anything could have happened to me."

"No," he said. "You're strong."

"I didn't feel strong," she said. "I felt helpless. Angry. I never want to feel like that again."

He pulled her into his lap on the bed and cradled her, pressing his lips to the top of her head in a gentle, soothing kiss. He seemed to understand now that what had hurt most wasn't just the cheating; it was the abandonment. And it was feeling like she was the one to blame because she'd known it should be too good to be true yet still blindly believed in it.

"I never should have moved for him."

"You did nothing wrong," he said, his voice clearly trying to contain the anger he was feeling over the Scott situation. "You did what a good woman would have, and if he'd been a good man, it would have been fine. That was his job, to be a good man. A trustworthy man. He failed at that." He held her tight. "I won't, Janna. I promise."

She leaned into him. She was tired of not being able to trust. Tired of planning to spend her life alone because she didn't want to be hurt again. Tired of Scott showing up at the store as if he thought he could take control of her life again just by stalking her.

"I'll protect you, Always," Ryder said in a low, growly voice. "With all parts of me."

She smiled and reached up to play with his hair. "All parts? Are there more than one?"

He smiled a half smile that didn't quite reach his eyes. "Maybe."

"Keeping secrets, hm?"

"Not that I want to," he said.

"Probably good, though," she said, stroking a hand down the side of his face. "I'm only just now getting used to the idea of you wanting me. I'll need some time to recover before you drop any other bombs on me."

He seemed to wince at that but hid it quickly. What was that?

"What is it?" she asked.

He opened his mouth to tell her but then looked up at the window across from her and his eyes went wide with shock. "Shit."

She flipped around, feeling a chill rush down her back as she turned to where he'd been looking. At the window, black eyes stared back at her. The bear from before. She screamed and pressed into Ryder as the bear reared up on its back legs and took a swipe at the window.

"Damn it," Ryder said. "The worst possible time. I should have known."

"Known what?" she asked, her heart trying to pound out of her chest as the window made a cracking noise and the bear reared back for another blow. It was monstrously huge, and she could feel how tense Ryder was behind her. Clearly, he was afraid of bears too. Who wasn't?

The sound of shattering glass made her scream again. The bear reached its giant paw through the window, scraping in her direction. Then it pulled out with a howl of pain and reared back again.

She tried to grab Ryder's arm, but before she could, he pulled out of her reach with a muttered apology. She looked into his eyes in disbelief as he left her alone on the bed. He gave her a look that said how sorry he was just as he reached the door. Then he ran through it, leaving her alone with the bear.

CHAPTER
THIRTEEN

SHE DIDN'T HAVE TIME TO feel her heart crack in two because the black bear had shattered more of the window. He reached both paws in and she grabbed a sheet to cover her nakedness as she tried to think what to do. She had only seconds. One more swipe and he'd probably be in. Dammit. Her body was limp, dizzy from the pleasure overload, not ready to go into fight mode, but she tried to drag herself from the bed and tripped.

The bear eyed her—she could swear it looked triumphant—and started to push its upper body through the window. Then its eyes widened and it howled in pain. The next second, it was gone, yanked back through the window by some unknown force.

She clutched the sheet around her and ran to the window. Outside, a tremendous brown bear with a shaggy pelt was fighting with the smaller black bear. The black bear didn't seem to stand a chance, and he knew it. One massive swipe from the grizzly bear had the black bear running away from the cabin. It sent her one last resentful stare over its shoulder, as if it were promising it would come back, and then disappeared over one of the snowy hills in the distance. Her heart was still pounding, even when the bear was out of sight.

She could have died if not for the other bear.

What was it with her and bears lately?

The grizzly looked over at her, roared with its head back, and then shook off snow and ran off in the opposite direction of the black bear. She almost wanted to thank it, but that was crazy. For all she knew, this bear wanted to eat her too. She crossed the bedroom to the other side of the cabin and looked out. The grizzly was disappearing into the trees.

She ran to her phone. She needed to call someone. Anyone. She had to get out of here. She knew Leslie wouldn't judge her for running. After she told her about the amazing Ryder Hart running away and leaving her naked and undefended, she'd be on her side for sure.

She didn't want him to come back and apologize. He'd just sound like Scott. She hadn't taken him for the kind of weak man that would hurt her and apologize later, like Scott was. But he'd sure acted like one. There was literally no good explanation for leaving her alone. He didn't take his phone. He didn't go for help, or if he had, he could have taken her. No, he'd just left her there like she meant nothing.

Right after he'd told her he loved her.

She dialed the number. No answer from Leslie. She tried Kylie. No pick up yet. Perhaps they were still driving down the canyon and didn't have reception. The incident with the bear had felt like forever but could have taken place in mere seconds.

It was late, and she was alone in the mountains. Ryder might come back, but how could she trust him not to run again? And she couldn't stay here with a broken window. The black bear might come back. The grizzly had weirdly seemed to be on her side, but the black bear... She knew it wouldn't stop until it got her. She didn't know why it wanted her, but it did.

There was one last number on her phone she could call. She had said she'd rather drop dead than ever ask him for help again, but she didn't actually want to die in a bear attack. And right now, facing Ryder would be worse. After what they'd just shared, how vulnerable she'd allowed herself to be with him…

At least Scott was who he was. A worm. And though he'd been a little persistent over the last year, he'd never actually touched or forced her. He was a weakling and a cheat, but he wouldn't make any move she couldn't rebuff. Not if he wanted another chance with her.

She reluctantly dialed the number as a cold gust of wind blew into the cabin through the open window.

"Scott?" she whispered when Scott picked up.

"Janna? What the hell?"

"I need a ride."

A pause on the other side. "Sure."

"And you better not try anything."

"Where are you?" he asked, sounding reasonable, like the Scott she'd first known.

"Up at the lodge."

"Ah. With him."

"Are you going to come get me or not?"

"I don't know. You've been ignoring me."

That was so Scott. Whiny and pathetic, but not threatening. "You owe me," she said simply, hoping he still felt at least a tinge of the guilt he should feel.

He sighed. "All right. But after this, you owe me."

She shook her head. If only her little town had cabs that weren't affiliated with the lodge. "Fine."

"A date?"

"Scott… don't push it. I'm in cabin number three."

"Fine," he said. "See you soon. I'm leaving now."

She hung up and set the phone on the bed, wondering when Ryder would come back in. What could he possibly say to excuse himself?

She got up, locked the bedroom door, pulled the curtains closed over the broken window, and changed into jeans and a sweatshirt. Then she began packing, shoving clothing haphazardly into her suitcase. When she was finished, she opened the door to the living room and picked up the clothing Ryder had scattered when he'd picked her up and started making love to her.

How they'd torn at each other's clothing. It was pure, hot passion. But it was nothing more if he could leave her like that.

He'd said he'd protect her. Well, she was a grown woman and she could deal. She'd already done it once. Honestly, driving home with Scott wouldn't be so bad after this. At least it would keep her mind off what a fool she'd been and the sheer shock she was still in that Ryder had run from the bear.

A part of her wanted to stay and listen to his explanation. But when she was fully packed and he hadn't returned, she decided she couldn't stay any longer. She sat on the couch and waited for Scott.

After a few moments, the door opened, and Ryder stood there.

Naked, his hair covered in snow.

She didn't even know what to say. On the one hand, his face had become familiar to her. The features beloved. And she wanted to rush into his arms and feel safe again.

On the other, the image of him running out of the room without a word was burned into her brain.

"Janna, we need to talk," he said, walking forward.

She took a deep breath, trying to calm her anger so she could stay cool and say what needed to be said. "About what? About how you left me after promising to protect me or about how you were apparently running around in the snow naked while I was in fear for my life?"

He blanched. "I know it looks bad, but I can explain."

She heard her voice grow slightly hysterical but couldn't stop it. "Oh really? Please do!" She waited, knowing there would be no explanation.

Ryder bit his lip and then shook his head and walked to the closet to pull out his travel case. He pulled on clothes, and she noticed he was shivering slightly. Well, too bad.

He walked forward as if to join her on the couch, but her furious expression stopped him dead in his tracks. She put up a hand.

"No, if you're going to explain, explain from there. I can't think when you're close."

One corner of his mouth almost quirked up at that, but he seemed to grasp the seriousness of the situation and what he'd done. She seriously hoped Scott drove slow so she'd get to hear whatever crazy story he came up with to excuse his actions. She could enjoy sharing it with the girls later.

"I..."

But a knock sounded at the door and Ryder turned toward it in shock. When he looked back at her, there was a hint of betrayal in those deep-blue eyes. "You called someone?"

She stood and grabbed her suitcase, fighting back tears. She didn't want to hurt him, but what could he expect? That she'd stay the rest of the week with him after that? No way. "Sorry, Ryder. I know you think I'm a strong woman, but I'm not that strong. This isn't going to work out."

He scratched at his head, ruffling the hair there furiously, still looking like he wanted to say something but knew it would sound crazy.

Well, he could keep his secrets. And she could go back to her ordinary life. It wasn't so bad compared to nearly being eaten by a bear.

"Don't leave," he said, walking forward to put his arms on hers. "You don't understand. You could be in danger."

She met his eyes. "Yeah, if I stayed with you."

"No, just give me a minute to explain. I have to show you."

"No," she said. "I have to go. Maybe I'll cool down later. Maybe at some point we can talk. But right now, I need to be home. Where I feel safe." She opened the door and Ryder sucked in his breath and let out a low curse when he saw Scott at the door.

"Not with him," he growled.

She felt her hackles rise and didn't see why he had any right to judge her. "Yes, him. He may be a cheat, but he'll get me home safe."

"Like hell," Ryder growled, coming between her and Scott. This display of protective dominance nearly made her knees weak again, but her rational mind was now firmly in the driver's seat and she wasn't letting it out again. She pushed hard on him, but he didn't budge.

"It's not your choice! You can't force me," she said.

At that, he let out a frustrated exhale and moved to the side. She walked to Scott, who put an arm around her waist. She let him. Not that she wanted him to, but she needed Ryder to get the hint and back off. At least for now. She needed to go cry it out somewhere where there were no bears and no confusing billionaires either.

"Wait," he said. "Just give me a minute to explain."

She clenched her suitcase. Everything in her body wanted to listen to him, wanted him to have a way to make it all okay. But she knew he couldn't. "You should have explained before you left me alone," she said.

Scott looked down at her curiously, but she just pulled away from him and walked out the door, dragging her suitcase behind her. Scott's truck was close by, and he loaded her luggage without a word and helped her into the passenger's seat.

Ryder came out into the snow in his bare feet, looking more like a desperate beggar than one of the most powerful men in the tech world. His blue eyes bored into hers, begging her not to go.

She turned away as Scott shut the door and refused to look up as they pulled away. She heard an angry roar and looked up to see Ryder had disappeared. Probably back into the cabin. He was good at running.

As they pulled out, she swore she saw the grizzly bear from before running across the white snow and back behind the lodge. It simply confirmed she'd made the right choice.

She leaned her cheek on her hand and rested her head against the frozen window, hoping Scott would just stay silent for the rest of the ride.

CHAPTER
FOURTEEN

RYDER RAN ANGRILY IN HIS bear form, wondering what he could have done differently while at the same time knowing there was nothing else he could have done.

He couldn't shift in the room with her. Even if he could get past the fear of telling her what he was, he knew there was a big risk that with his huge bear there, she could get hurt. And he wouldn't be able to get out the small window once in bear form. Or the bedroom door. And he would have wasted precious time having to lumber around to the back.

No, the best, quickest thing to do, instinctively, was run and change as quickly as possible so he could get the bear away from the window and keep his mate safe.

Damn! He'd been so close. She'd been opening her heart to him, trusting him, and now she thought he was the worst kind of man. Even worse than she probably could have imagined to be fearful of.

He hadn't thought about how it would look. He'd simply thought about what would be safest for her and done it, hoping he could explain afterward.

Oh, how he'd wanted to kill that stupid bear who dared to threaten her. But he knew it could traumatize her to watch him take it apart. So he'd simply chased it away and then patrolled the cabin until the scent had faded completely and the bear was far gone.

By the time he'd gotten back in, it had been too late. Oh, how the triumph of protecting her had faded when he'd seen the hate in her eyes. How it had stabbed him in the gut to see she'd immediately turned back to the man that hurt her in the beginning.

He'd wanted to charge the car and slash the tires and carry his mate inside and make love to her until she listened. But he couldn't. It would only hurt things between them more.

She'd said maybe they could talk later. If only he didn't go mad worrying about her in the meantime.

He wasn't worried about Scott. Jealous, yes. Angry, yes. But he'd seen nothing about the man that said he was going to take advantage. If anything, he'd seemed a little afraid of Ryder. Understandably. He was coming between him and his mate at a time when Ryder needed to protect her.

And Scott had no chance of it. When he'd smelled him while fresh from his bear form, he'd known. There was no bear in Scott. So what would he and Janna do if the black bear decided to follow them back to town and pay a visit to them there?

He growled and slashed at a tree when he thought of the possibility of Scott *not* taking her home. Maybe she wouldn't want to be alone tonight.

But damn it, she had to know better than that, didn't she? Scott could be nice, he was sure, but in the end, he'd still be the weakling that broke her heart. At least Ryder only broke her heart while trying to protect her life.

Even now, he couldn't regret what he'd done because he'd rather she was unharmed and angry at him than hurt. Angry, he could fix.

Even if the jealous, possessive animal inside him almost wanted to give up now that it looked like she'd chosen another male. Almost. In reality, every part of him wanted to fight. Fight until she was safe, fight until she was his, and fight until she was back in his arms.

He huffed as he ran down the road where they'd gone, trying to retain his human reasoning. He was Ryder Hart. Shrewd. Powerful. He made grown men tremble in boardrooms. He could control this. He could.

But his bear was still charging down the road, following the scent of the truck his mate had left in, staying just far enough out of sight not to scare her by letting her see him.

What he planned to do when he caught up, he didn't know. He just knew that every part of him needed to see her safe. A little ways down the road, he stopped.

His head started to clear, and the scent of the truck was fading. When he did see Janna again, he needed to be Ryder, not a bear. A bear would only scare her. And yes, he would have to show her his bear; it was the only way things would make sense and she would know he hadn't left her. But not yet. First, he needed to know she could give him a chance as a man.

Jealousy dug deep into his chest and he fought the transformation back into a man. Nothing good could come of wandering naked in the woods right now. He ran as fast as his legs could carry him, which was very fast, back to the cabin and hurriedly transformed and changed into his clothes when he got inside the living room. Then he put on boots, grabbed his phone, and ran to the lodge.

He unlocked the phone as he ran, dialing the first number that came to mind.

"Ryder?" Riley's voice was groggy, slurred. "What's up, man? It's late."

"I need a guy on surveillance," he snapped, hoping his brother would immediately catch the seriousness of his tone.

"Whoa, okay. Why?"

"I need one of your bodyguards. Can you spare him?"

"Sure, what happened? You okay? Where are you? I can come out."

"I'm headed to the lodge. Almost there."

"I'll see you in a minute."

Ryder reached the side door to the huge lodge at the same time Riley opened it for him. His younger brother drew him into a bear hug and held on tight, then released him. Ryder bristled at the contact. Not all bears liked hugs.

"Where's Mike?" he snapped.

"He's getting dressed. I don't have them on duty when I'm just at the bar."

"Why did you bring them, then?"

Riley shrugged. "You never know."

Ryder put a hand to his face and sighed. "Fine. I'll write down the address. I need someone outside. Watching for bears, in particular." Since Mike was a highly trained wolf shifter, Ryder knew he could handle it.

Riley raised an eyebrow, finally grasping the seriousness of the situation. "Bears? Or bear shifters?"

"I think you know," Ryder said.

"Shit," Riley said. "Janna?"

Ryder nodded. "I had to leave her to transform. A bear attacked the window. She thought…"

"She thought you ran away!" Riley's eyes widened and he barked out a laugh. "That's hilarious." At Ryder's scowl, he frowned and shook his head. "I mean, it would be if it hadn't blown everything to shit, right?"

Ryder just glared.

"All right, Mike'll be on the job. How long do you want him?"

"No more than a couple days. I'm giving her space so she can cool down, and then I'll talk to her."

Riley sighed and put a hand on his brother's shoulder. Ryder glared at it, and he removed it. "Look, you know women don't actually want that, right?"

"What do you mean?"

"I mean they hate when you give them space. When they say they need space, they usually want you to chase them. Sometimes they'll get mad if you don't."

Ryder scoffed. "That's absurd. Why would I go against what she wants?"

"Because she's wrong and you know it. And it hurts her to be thinking the wrong thing, and you can correct it for her."

"She wouldn't talk to me. Hell, I don't blame her. I don't know what I would have done differently. I should have explained or something. I should have taken a second to tell her. Anything but just run out of the house and have her see me walk in a few minutes later, totally naked."

"That does look weird, bro. All the more reason to track her down and make her see the truth."

Ryder raised an eyebrow. "See, but that's the thing with dating humans. I can't just show up and intimidate her with my bear. It'd scare her."

"More than seeing you run away from a fight to play naked in the woods? Nah, I don't think so."

When had his brother gotten so wise about women? Practice made perfect maybe, he thought skeptically. But he couldn't deny Riley might be right about Janna. "What do I do?"

"Now *that* I don't know. I'll send Mike down there, but I'd get your ass down there as soon as possible."

"Tonight?" he asked.

Riley shrugged. "I don't know. Might be smart to let her get some sleep. How did she get back down?"

"Her ex," Ryder said, blurting it out through a lump in his throat.

"Damn!" Riley exclaimed. "She threw you aside fast. You sure you want this one?"

Ryder's expression darkened. "I *only* want this one. I'm going to fix this."

"Sure, bro," Riley said, shaking his head. "But how, I don't know."

"I'm an alpha," Ryder said. "I'll figure it out."

"Sure." Riley placed the call to Mike and then slipped his phone back in his pocket. "But maybe you'll want to get down there and stay somewhere in town. So you're close in case she needs you. And so you can see if the ex takes her home or to his place."

Ryder felt his bear rise up inside him. He wouldn't let that happen. Scott would only take advantage of her and hurt her again. He liked to think Janna would never go for it, but he'd left her hurt and probably feeling vulnerable.

Still, he'd tear Scott apart before he let him touch her.

But what if Janna *wanted* Scott to touch her? The thought made him nearly lose control of his bear right there.

But then he took a deep breath and summoned the rational mind that had made him who he was. In this fight for his mate, brain would be just as important as brawn.

And his brain combined with his passion had never let him down.

"I'm going down there. But I still want Mike."

"Sure thing. I'll text him your number. He can keep you updated. Where will you stay?"

"I'm not sure," he said. "I'll sleep in the woods if I have to." He turned to go and then stopped and put a hand on Riley's shoulder. Riley looked shocked at the contact. Ryder shrugged. "Thanks for the help."

"Sure thing," Riley said. "And Ryder?"

"Yes?"

"I smelled it too. She's at least part bear. That's why she's having so much trouble. When you tell her, at least a small part of her should accept what you say as the truth."

"I hope so," Ryder said, turning to go.

"What will you do if she doesn't?" Riley called after him.

Ryder looked at his brother over his shoulder. "I'll negotiate."

At that, Riley went completely silent and then barked out a laugh.

Ryder went back to the cabin, packed, and then got in his Range Rover and headed out into the snow-blurred night.

He'd be there for his mate whether she wanted him or not. And then he'd make her see she was meant for him, by whatever means necessary.

WHEN THEY ARRIVED BACK AT her place, Scott helped Janna out and followed her up to the door.

Now for the awkward part, she thought.

She gave him an awkward hug, which he barely returned, but he still didn't leave.

"What happened?" he asked.

She folded her arms over her chest and looked down. "I don't want to talk about it. Look, Scott, I appreciate you picking me up, but after you hurt me, I'm not really interested in anything further with you."

He sighed. "I didn't mean to hurt you. You were the best thing that happened to me. I guess I just… wasn't thinking."

She set down her suitcase with an exasperated sigh. "You were thinking, all right. You were thinking with your other head, and now you regret it because she left."

He frowned, pouting. "Look, can't we let bygones be bygones? You're not the woman I cheated on. You've been getting stronger every day. I can tell. When you called me, I thought you were ready to bury the hatchet."

"No," she said, shocked he could even think that. "I don't know if I'll ever be ready to bury the hatchet. Do you know what you did to me, Scott? How hard you made it for me to trust men after that?"

He scowled. "Apparently not enough for you to not run off with that Ryder guy. I guess money talks, huh, Janna?"

She frowned. "That's none of your business. I'm not yours anymore. I'm not sure if I ever was."

"You were mine," he said, and the wistful look on his face almost made her heart twinge with a bit of regret for how things had happened. But they couldn't go back. Even if she was learning to let other men in, she couldn't with him. She'd be stupid to.

Maybe some people could overcome cheating. Especially if the partner confessed. But she'd caught him, and he'd stayed with the other woman as long as he could.

He only came back to Janna when she was the only option.

At least Ryder had treated her like the first option. He hadn't come on to any of her friends. Well, she didn't know what he'd done when she wasn't around, but he'd been around her pretty much since he'd gotten into town.

Nothing made sense. From the minute he'd met her, he'd been protective, brave, strong. Why did he run?

But her heart sank as she wondered if she was simply trying to find a way to let him off the hook. Or was it just that her intuition kept saying there was more to it than met the eye?

She couldn't tell and she was too tired to do it right now, with Scott on her porch.

"Good night," she said. Then she turned, unlocked the door, and went inside, not waiting for Scott to protest.

The apartment was dark and a little cold. She'd turned the heat down before she left.

Everything here was so familiar. Knickknacks she'd had since she was little littered the fireplace mantle. The small living room had a couch, a worn but practical rug, and a comfy chair by the window where she could read. There were still books strewn across the seat.

She walked to the chair and slumped down in it. She picked up one of the romance novels she'd been reading previously and leafed through it.

Book romance was a little unsatisfying after being so close to the real thing. She bit her lip and closed the book, setting it on her lap. Then her eye locked onto something outside, and she sat up a little, staring out.

There was an unfamiliar car parked on the other side of the road. The windows were tinted so she couldn't see inside. A shudder of fear went through her, and she remembered the phone message. She stood to look out the window. Scott's truck was gone. Supposedly, he'd gone home with his tail between his legs.

She was proud of herself for standing up to him. She could remember a Janna who wouldn't have. Who would have begged him to come back. But she knew she was worth more now. Ryder had made her feel that way.

But then he'd run. But that didn't change the things he'd said or the way he'd only had eyes for her or the way he made her melt in his arms.

Her brain searched for something that would make everything fit, but she could sense that whatever it was, the answer was just beyond the realm of her comprehension.

So she continued to watch the SUV, letting the fear keep her awake. She'd known the person who left that message wasn't Scott. It just didn't fit him.

She checked the clock over the mantle. Midnight. Still too late to call Leslie or Kylie, but she hated being alone. Any of her other friends she'd made in the town had kids and couldn't be woken.

Maybe it was time to get a cat.

Or go crawling back to Ryder, willing to accept he was a fraidy-cat who liked to run away from bears.

But she knew that was probably just the tiredness talking. She decided nothing was happening in the SUV that she should worry about. Nothing she could do either way. Someone was probably just visiting family. She stood, checked the deadbolt, turned off the lights, and headed upstairs.

She turned on her bedroom light and slowly changed, taking clothes off her aching body. Both the adrenaline of the bear attack and the ardent love Ryder had made to her had tired her out.

But she knew which she preferred. She thought of his large hands smoothing over her body, heating her skin as he whispered sweet words. She changed into soft pajamas and lay there for a few minutes, touching her own skin and wishing it felt like it did when Ryder touched her.

Why couldn't she stop thinking of him, even when he'd proven her worst fears to be true?

She guessed, as with Scott, it would take time. But she had the feeling it would take a lot longer with Ryder than it did with Scott.

There were moments with Ryder she was sure she would always remember.

On that thought, and a few others about their time together, she fell into weary sleep.

CHAPTER
FIFTEEN

WHEN SHE WOKE, EVERYTHING SEEMED clearer. The sun streaming through the icy patterns on the window lit up the room and cast light over the bed. She pushed hair out of her eyes and let out a long sigh. She stood, pulled on a robe, and walked to the window to look down. The SUV was still there, but nothing out of place seemed to have happened.

She checked her phone. No messages.

Did she want Ryder to call? She didn't know. She'd told him she needed to cool off. Was that true?

She put a hand to her head. She already felt better this morning. Ready to talk, ready to forgive. But then the shock, the fear of being left alone all came rushing back. And he'd done it right after she'd told him how much Scott had hurt her. Right after he'd promised not to abandon her.

Maybe that's why he'd said it was the worst possible time. Because he knew showing his cowardly side at that moment would ruin things.

But that just didn't seem like the Ryder she knew. She walked down into the kitchen and turned on the coffee maker. She'd need about a gallon to feel conscious after the night she'd had. Maybe she'd let Sherry run the store this week anyway. Take a much-needed vacation. She'd bet Leslie would be up for traveling somewhere fun, and Kylie too if she didn't sub any other days this week.

But Ryder…

She couldn't stop thinking of him. Of how incredible the night had been before it'd gone bad. Of him asking her to spend her life with him. Him saying he loved her. But how was that possible with what came after?

A knock on the door interrupted her thoughts. Ryder? She ran to the door to open it, knowing it was foolish how quickly her heart leapt at the thought of seeing him but eager to work things out between them.

There had to be a way to explain it. There just had to. Part of being rational was knowing when something didn't add up and the only rational thing to do is look into it until it does.

There's always a reason if you're brave enough to find it.

Ryder was worth the chance, and he'd certainly put himself out there for her emotionally after they'd made love.

She yanked open the door and gasped when she saw not Ryder, but Barry. Ryder's father's embezzling accountant. His graying hair was slicked in a comb over, and there were dark circles under his eyes.

"Barry!" she exclaimed, pulling her robe tightly closed, glad her pajamas underneath were thick and full length, covering everything but her hands and feet. "What are you doing here? I thought you'd left town."

"And leave you here to tell everyone what a screw-up I was?" he asked, pushing his way past her and inside before she could block the entrance. Dammit, after this, she was installing a peephole on her door whether her landlord okayed it or not.

Still, the short man didn't scare her. He was barely 5'10", just slightly taller than her but much smaller due to being skinnier. If he aggravated her, she could probably sit on him. After seeing what he'd done to Ryder's family, she'd be happy to.

"I've been going over your records, yes," she said, holding the door open and gesturing for him to go out. "We can talk at my office if you want. Later."

He eyed her warily. He was wearing worn, faded gray sweats over his bony body, and he looked like he hadn't eaten or slept enough lately. He looked… slightly feral.

"Fine," he said. "When?"

She looked at the kitchen clock. Anything to get Barry out of here so she could get ready. "How about in an hour?"

"Perfect," he said. "You still at the same place?"

"Of course," she said, lifting her chin. She didn't like the way he was leering at her as he left.

"See you then," he muttered, and she took great pleasure in slamming the door behind him.

She sighed and looked at the clock again. No time for coffee. She needed a nice long shower and to get dressed and get her hair back in control. She'd pick something up after meeting with Barry. Not that she expected much to come of the meeting, but at least it'd be safer out in public. Not that Barry would hurt her. But she had some pretty unpleasant things to say to him about Ryder's family business and how he'd treated it, and she wanted witnesses if something went wrong.

Barry looked like a man with nothing to lose.

She climbed the stairs to her bedroom, looked at the phone again, saw there were no messages, and took the phone into the bathroom, putting it on the counter while she showered.

The heat was hypnotic and relaxing, but throughout the shower and getting ready after, all she could think about was Ryder. His hands, his eyes. That body. It was like he had bewitched her utterly.

She was still in kind of a fog, unsure what to do about the Ryder situation, feeling like her brain was just on the brink of a breakthrough about it when she headed out the door to meet Barry. She kept her phone close at hand in her pocket and wore a heavy trench that concealed her body. She hadn't liked the way Barry looked at her.

This was exactly the kind of meeting she would have wanted to go to with Ryder. He was probably ace at negotiations and difficult discussions. It was the difference between a simple accountant and someone who made billions. That hard edge she knew she'd never have. She was too soft.

But Ryder could be soft too, when the time called for it. He'd been so gentle. Contrasted with his hard side, the in-control side, the plunging-into-her-while-uttering-oaths-of-wonder side, she wasn't sure which she loved more.

And that was it. The whole problem. She loved him. As improbable as it was that he could love her after this short time, she was fairly certain, in an animal way deep down inside her, that she loved him back. And didn't that leave her in a funny position?

She kept her head down as she walked down the street toward her shop. But between buildings, at a place where the woods bordered the street, someone jumped out, startling her.

"Barry!" she said, taking a step away from him. "I thought we were meeting at the store."

"We were," he said, eyes narrowing. "I had a change of plans."

Her stomach coiled in response and she gingerly put one hand in her pocket to feel for her phone, making sure it was still there and she could dial it in a moment's notice. "I'd really rather meet up at the office. I was looking forward to my morning walk. Alone." She emphasized the last word and his expression seemed to darken.

"Fine," he said, and he walked ahead of her and disappeared around a corner.

"Phew." She breathed a sigh of relief and kept walking, this time at a brisker pace. She didn't want to talk to him here. It'd be too easy for him to pull her off into the woods. Not that he had any reason to, but she just felt nervous around him.

Her heart sank and she brushed her fingers over the phone again. Had Barry left the threatening message? Because he knew if she stayed at the lodge, she'd expose him? If so, Barry was stupid if he thought Janna was the real threat. Ryder was equally capable with numbers and was clearly on to him. She shrugged, shook her head, and kept walking, but then something darted out, bit down on the back of her coat, and yanked her viciously off the path.

She screamed but was cut off when the animal brutishly jerked her around. It dragged her, stunned, into the woods, and Janna was grateful for her thick coat that protected her from the cold ground and the protruding sticks.

"Let me go!" she said, struggling against the hold on her coat that had it pulled up, almost choking her. "What are you doing?" She craned her neck and gasped when she realized it was a bear holding her. Shit! The bear from the window. "No!"

She thrashed her arms, and the bear ignored her, dragging her farther into the woods where she doubted anyone would hear her.

Even Barry, who might have been close enough to help a minute ago, probably couldn't hear her now. If she could even scream when the coat was cutting off her air.

"Can't... breathe," she choked out, and the bear went a few feet and then dropped her. She yanked at her collar, pulling the coat down and preparing to scream, but the bear got in her face, snarling and snapping its jaws viciously in warning. Each time she dared open her mouth, it did it again.

She cringed away, heart stammering. But because this was her third encounter with the bear, she was determined to try and stay calm. After all, her life depended on it.

The bear paced in front of her, somehow satisfied as long as she seemed afraid. It wasn't hard. The teeth in that massive jaw could easily tear her apart. Thinking about it was... not enjoyable.

"What do you want?" she asked. She somehow sensed this was no regular bear, and even though her rational mind knew there was no point talking to animals, she knew it couldn't hurt. And rational thinking didn't exactly apply to being stalked and kidnapped by a bear who didn't seem to want to eat her.

Why would it want her, then?

Then the bear stopped, eyeing her, and she swore she could see hunger in those deep, dark depths. But not for food. She opened her mouth in shock, and the bear roared, raising a paw as if to strike her. She put up a hand to block her face and winced, bracing for the blow. This was it. There was nothing she could do.

She wouldn't even get to say good-bye to Ryder. To find out his mystery.

The blow never came. Instead, with a roar, a large, brown, shaggy mass flew at the black bear, knocking it away from her and wrestling it to the ground. It was the grizzly from the night before. Though it was twice the size of the black bear and truly a terrifying, ferocious sight, for some reason, all she could feel was relief at its presence. She scrambled back as the bears fought, roaring and slashing at each other.

She wanted to look away, but she couldn't tear her eyes away from the scene. She knew that her life depended on who won.

Luckily, it was over fairly quickly. The black bear was in submission and trying to crawl away, and the grizzly had him pinned with one paw. The black bear winced as the grizzly raised his other paw to finish the job, and then, as if something were blurring in front of her eyes, the black bear changed. She blinked and nearly missed it but could swear that black bear had just twisted and transformed into a man.

Barry. Naked.

Her eyes went wide as saucers and she covered her them as the grizzly bear let out an angry roar.

"You can't kill me while I'm human," Barry stammered weakly.

Her heart pounded and her brain struggled to comprehend his words. While he was human? She looked at the grizzly.

The grizzly looked angry, frustrated by Barry's cowardice, but it stepped back to let him go. Barry put his hands up as the bear stared down at him.

"I'm going. I promise. I didn't think she was your mate. I thought you were just playing with her. I'm not stupid enough to come between a grizzly and his mate. But I didn't think you'd take a human with so little bear in her..."

The grizzly roared, and Janna felt lightheaded at what she was hearing. But the weirdest was yet to come.

"Mess with my mate again, and I'll make you wish you were never born. Human or not!"

Janna recognized that low, growly voice. But had never heard it sound so angry.

"Ryder?" she asked, wondering where he was hiding. Why was he somewhere in the woods when she was being attacked by a bear?

The bear looked at her with something like guilt in its ageless eyes. Eyes that were shadowed by a long, shaggy pelt but nevertheless looked right into her soul with a piercing shade of sapphire blue.

What. The. Hell?

"I'm sorry, honey," the bear said, mouth moving unnaturally.

That's it. She was hallucinating. She scooted back another step, then looked over at Barry as he took advantage of the bear's attention on her to run screaming from the scene.

Somehow, she didn't think they'd have to worry about him anymore.

"Don't be scared," the bear said, coming closer. "It's me."

Her heart stammered wildly and she let out a little squeak as she scrambled back. Then the bear blurred in front of her face, as the other had done before Barry appeared, and she found herself looking at a pair of large, naked thighs.

Ryder sighed and dropped to crouch in front of her, eye to eye. "I'm sorry, honey. I tried to tell you."

Her head went light. "Oh, so you're the bear," she said weakly, barely certain if the words were coming from her own mouth at this point.

He nodded.

"Ah," she said faintly. "That makes sense."

Then she fainted dead away.

CHAPTER
SIXTEEN

WHEN JANNA WOKE UP, SHE was back in her bedroom. It was bright outside, with shards of light penetrating the curtains drawn closed at her window. But it was dark in the room. The light was off, and a shadowy figure was sitting next to her bed on a chair brought up from kitchen.

The figure was tall, dark-haired, and familiar.

"Ryder?" she said, sitting up and rubbing her head. Her hair was frizzy and out of control, and she fumbled on her nightstand for a hair band and pulled it into a rough ponytail. Then she flicked the switch to turn on the lamp. "What are you doing here?" She sighed. "I had the weirdest dream."

Then she noticed the scratches on his face, the dirt on his clothing.

Maybe it wasn't a dream.

"I should have told you sooner," he said quietly. "I'm usually a good strategist. Completely in control. Able to execute a plan just the way I want. But that all went out the window when it came to you."

"Didn't you think I'd want to know you were a bear before I started dating you?" she asked quietly. Then she shook her head. When *was* a good time to spring that on someone? "I mean, at least after we were intimate the first time, you could have mentioned it."

"And you wouldn't have run away screaming?" he asked quietly, his handsome face calm and resigned. "Don't lie. You fainted when you saw me. But I couldn't help it at that point. I had to shift or you would think another bear was threatening you."

"So you were the grizzly bear outside the window?" she asked, putting a hand up to her lips. "Oh my gosh, I'm so sorry. Thank you for saving me."

"Of course," he said seriously.

She put her hands over her face. "What a mess."

"It was bad luck, I admit." He shrugged. "All I was thinking about was how to keep you safe. And now that you've seen my grizzly up close, you see why me shifting in that tiny room would have been a bad idea. My claws could have caught you."

She nodded, trying to calm the part of her that kept screaming this shouldn't be possible, that she must be dreaming. But she wasn't. She had clearly just woken up. And Ryder Hart was really in front of her, flesh and blood, talking about being able to turn into a bear.

"Your brothers, are they like you?"

He nodded.

"Oh my gosh. The world's hottest movie star is a freaking bear."

"I wouldn't call him the hottest," Ryder said. "For now, he seems to be doing well with the romantic roles. But the world is fickle that way."

"Maybe," she said. "But that doesn't change that he's a bear. A freaking bear."

His jaw twitched. "And what's wrong with bears?" He took a deep breath and relaxed back on the chair, long legs stretched in front of him as he folded his arms. "Never mind. Honestly, if I was more used to shifting, I probably could have handled the situation better. In a way that made you feel safe but still kept you safe. But I'm a city bear. I panicked and I let my bear take over. And he just wanted to go out and beat off the bear that was threatening you. Bears fight for mates, you know."

She nodded. Did she know that? How much did she really know about bears? How much did she think about them?

"So how often are you a bear?" she asked. "Like, do you have to live as one sometimes?"

He shrugged. "I would think not. I haven't had a lot of bear time growing up in Silicon Valley. I remember shifting more when I was little. When Dad was around to take us out into the wilderness."

"What happened that made you move?"

Ryder flinched, and she almost wished she hadn't asked the question. But if she was going to open up with him, she needed to know all she could.

"My mother died in a car accident. I don't even know what caused it. I was on the computer, messing around like usual. I was a prodigy even then, better with electronics than people. More interested in making money than making friends. But I heard Riley's scream. I came downstairs. Dad was standing there."

"I'm so sorry," she said, knowing the words were wholly inadequate but knowing with grieving people, sometimes it was best to just apologize and let them speak.

"Dad wasn't around a lot. I think we blamed him. We hadn't seen him for a week when he came home with the news. He hadn't been with her when it happened. The police had called him."

"Where was he?"

Ryder pressed his firm lips together and sat forward with clasped hands. "My dad was raised in a different generation. Bear shifters were getting so rare; there was a lot of pressure to mate with as many people as possible. Rather than take one life mate. It wasn't until I read the letter in his will that I understood."

"So he was off cheating?" She dropped her jaw but pulled it back up with some effort. Ryder didn't need her judgment right now. He'd clearly struggled with this for years. "Sorry, what did the letter say?"

"It said not to make the same mistake. That we should try and find happiness at Bearstone Park, like he did, but this time, not mess it up."

"And you all agreed to come?"

"He was our father. Of course we did. Bears may be solitary creatures, but they are loyal. In the wild, there's never enough food for them to travel together. But when they see each other, they are often happy to cuddle or greet one another. When my mother died, my father finally realized everything that had been told him was wrong. He knew he should have mate claimed my mother. But you have to understand, back when he was growing up, only wolves mate claimed. Bears were considered too rare and encouraged to be promiscuous, like they were in the wild."

"Mate claim? What's that?" she asked, feeling a prickle of anticipation at the thought.

"It's when a shifter claims a mate, essentially saying she's his for life and he's hers alone. I think my father knew my mother was his mate, but he fought it, trying to do his duty while keeping her happy as much as he could."

"How did she cope with that?"

"Well, I think she knew she was the one he loved. I liked to think that. She never showed us a sad face. She probably kept that to herself. When they were together, they were truly happy. And she had us."

"Hm, I see," she said, thinking if Ryder meant to propose something like that, she'd tell him where he could stick his promiscuity.

"But in that letter he wrote me in his will, he said he knew what a mistake it all had been. He'd lived an unhappy life, away from his mate when she truly needed him. When he could have been protecting her. And she was the only one that ended up giving him children anyway."

"So you want me to have your kids?" she asked skeptically. "I don't even know if I want that. At least not yet."

He shook his head. "Just listen. Look, I realized what my dad said when I first laid eyes on you. And from then on, I was destined to follow you, just like a male bear would follow a female in the wild. You were the one. I knew it when I saw you, just like my dad knew it when he saw my mom."

"How?" she asked. "Is this what you meant when you said you knew in some special part of you that we were made for each other? How did you know?"

He shook his head, and his dark hair fluttered, catching the morning light. The sight made her catch her breath. The fact that everything had been crazy didn't change the good times they had together. The times everything felt right. And how undeniably handsome he was. She just needed to hear a little more before she made a decision.

Even if her heart was already leaning toward Ryder.

"What do you want from me?" she asked when he didn't answer.

"All of you," he said gravely, meeting her eyes with his intent sapphire irises. "Is that too much to ask?" He laughed hoarsely and sat up in his chair. "As for how I knew… I just did. I can't explain it. The same way I know what to invest in and what to sell. Instinct, but on a much stronger, deeper level. I thought my dad was full of it when he talked about love at first sight, but I knew how wrong I was when I saw you."

"That's ridiculous," she said as much at her own joyful response to his admission as to his declaration itself.

He moved forward, taking her hand. It nearly disappeared in his huge fingers and made her think of other places she'd felt that warm, comforting touch. "Do I really seem like a flippant man to you? Do I seem like the type that would completely abandon my work to go after just any woman? Do I seem like the type that would make love to her, say I love her, and ask her to spend her life with me, all for a lay?"

She frowned. That was true. But even though she now knew he wasn't a coward, her heart was still trying to move into untrusting mode. "How do I know you won't be like your dad?" she asked.

"Because I'll mate claim you. The mate claim is a serious promise. It means that I die when you die, and it means I never mate with another. And you don't either."

"Sort of like marriage for humans?" she asked.

"Yes, but more serious," he said. "Mate claims are no joke in the bear world. Especially since there have been relatively few cases of it. We've known how to do it but haven't wanted to for many years because we were afraid the race was dying out. But if it's going to die out anyway, we may as well be happy. Honestly, I didn't care if the race died out if it was the reason my mom and dad fell apart."

"Understandable," she said, feeling a prickle of excitement for what was coming. "So how do you mate claim?"

"It's a little complicated," he said. "It's two part."

"Okay, what is it?"

He shook his head, kissed her hand, and placed it back on her knee. Then he stood and placed a hand on either side of her on the bed. "I can't tell you yet. Not until you agree."

"How can I possibly decide now?" she asked.

"You've seen my bear. You know me as a man. And since there's some bear in you, I suspect you already know inside how you feel about me, even if it feels a little ridiculous."

She did. She swallowed, embarrassed he could see it. She pulled the covers higher.

His gaze bored into her. "So I'll tell you again. What I told you the other night, that you seemed to be okay with. I love you, Janna. You're it for me. I know you think it matters that I'm a billionaire, but it doesn't. As far as you're concerned, I'm just a dumb bear who has found the bear for him and will have his heart broken if you say no."

She looked up at him, her heart welling with love.

"So, Janna, what's your answer?"

CHAPTER
SEVENTEEN

HER FROZEN HEART WAS MELTING all over the place, and she resisted the urge to reach out to him as love started to overflow. She wanted to hear everything he had to say first. He could be so sweet when he wanted to.

She reached up and touched the dimple in his cheek, rubbed a thumb over the slight cleft in his chin, and smiled at him.

He blushed, right over his cheekbones. "So, Janna, do you love me? Will you take this crazy step and say yes to spending your life with me? You now know I'll do anything to protect you. I'll fight anything that threatens you. I'll always be there for you. The rest are just details. We can make a life together if you just say yes."

She looked up into his eyes. "But where would we live?"

"Anywhere we want. If you want to live here and stay by your friends, I can work remotely. I kind of like the idea of raising a family here." When he saw she was about to interrupt, he raised a hand to her lips gently. "Even if that family is just you and me."

"I can't make any promises," she said. "What if one of us changes our minds?"

He drew back and rose to his full height. Commanding, powerful. "I'm never going to change my mind because my bear has never felt like this. And I know from my father that he never will. And the human in me sees even more than the bear does. Knows rationally what the bear can't explain. You're smart. You're beautiful. You're giving and cautious, but you keep on trying and putting yourself out there. You're warm and loving and awesome in bed. I love your body. I love everything about you, Janna. Time won't change that."

She swallowed, closed her eyes, and listened deep inside herself. She could feel the forest. When he'd said she was part bear, she'd been too stunned by everything else to ask about it. But it made sense. Was that why she'd been so intrigued by the thought of coming out here? If there was bear in her, it was just very slight. But she could still feel that part calling out to him, telling the human part of her to listen. That this was a mate that was one in a million, and she should snap him up and work out the details later.

And anyone looking at Ryder Hart or who knew anything about this probably would say the same thing.

"Yes," she said, standing up to hug him. His strong arms enclosed her in a tight hug, and she coughed. "Now I know why they call it a bear hug," she gasped out.

"Yeah," he said, not letting go. "Although, you know in the wild, a bear hug is an awful thing. Clawing, fighting…"

"Shhh," she said, hugging him close, luxuriating in his warmth and the fact that although this should have been too good to be true, she knew it was actually true. She knew it deep inside herself, with that instinctive part she'd never listened to before. She'd definitely not had that feeling about Scott.

No part of her worried about things with Ryder. She knew he'd take care of her and she'd care for him, and the rest was just getting to know each other.

"So you'll really accept this bear who's a billionaire?" he asked, running a hand through her hair, placing a kiss to her neck, holding her tightly around the waist.

"I suppose," she said. "What's next?"

He stepped back. "I hadn't thought about that. I mean, I know you're going to be mine. But the timeline can be flexible. I just needed to know you'd be an eventual mate, because only humans who are mates can see us in bear form. Otherwise, we're supposed to wipe their memory."

"How do you do that?" she asked fearfully.

He pulled her in tight again. "Don't worry. I'm not letting anyone do that to you. But I would definitely have to leave and not tell you any more about our customs. And that would break my heart, so thanks for not making that necessary."

"No problem," she said, laughing. "Thanks for rescuing me from a life of boring solitude."

"Ha!" he said, teasing her. "I doubt your life could ever be boring. That's part of what I like about you. You seek adventure. You just do it in different ways from other people. After all, you agreed to go work with a billionaire for a week."

"I did."

"Even though you probably suspected the billionaire had fairly… untoward motives." He dipped his head to kiss her neck again and then her ear, and a little thrill shot through her.

"So this mate claiming process," she murmured as he licked along the inner shell of her ear. "Does it involve actual mating?"

"It can, but not exactly. Do you want to know?" he asked quietly, his lips tickling her ear. Her knees went weak and he held her up.

She nodded.

He laughed, a low, husky voice that affected her down to her toes.

"All right." He whispered it into her ear, and her eyes widened.

"That's it? Seriously?"

"Hey, it's pretty complicated when you factor in the whole telling a human you're a bear thing. The rest is easy. Well, if they don't run away screaming first."

"I can do that," she said. "I could do it now if you wanted."

He shook his head. "There's something I want to do first. The human part of me."

"Okay," she said. "What's that?"

"A surprise," he said. "I can't do it now. I'll have to do it later."

"Fine," she said, entwining her hands around his neck. "As long as you do something I want right now."

He leaned back to look at her, eyes flaring with heat. "Oh, really?"

"Yes," she said, moving her hand down the front of his pants to cup him. "Really."

He groaned and pushed her back onto the bed. "Are you sure you're ready for this? It's been a rough day."

"I know," she said, nipping his ear as he leaned over her. "That's why I need the stress relief."

"Any excuse to get your hands on my body?" he asked, smirking.

She laughed. "Yes."

"Fine by me," he said. "I've been unable to think of anything else since I met you. Well, I mean, I've been thinking of how to keep bears off of you and how to tell you I was a bear, but I was—"

"Ryder?" she said, looking up at him.

"Yes?"

"Shut up and take me."

He let out a curse and then grinned at her. "Yes, ma'am."

"That's right," she said, laughing and wrapping her arms around his neck.

And he did. Slowly, luxuriously kissing every part of her like it was the first time all over again. Like everything was new because she was his now. She'd agreed to it, acknowledged it. The lovemaking was warm with the security of commitment, with the knowledge that he'd fought for her, twice. That he'd never abandoned her, but actually been right there with her.

That he'd been vulnerable to her.

So she made herself vulnerable to him, opening completely and accepting him in. And when she did, he groaned in pleasure and murmured words of uninhibited love in her ear, which she answered without reservation.

Just two people in love, against the odds, a woman and her bear, tangled up in the sheets in the ecstasy of passion. And then it was over and they held each other close, both wondering how anyone could ever be so lucky.

"I love you, Janna," Ryder said, stroking her hair as she lay against his chest. "I'll always love you. You know that, right?"

"Yes," she said.

"And?"

She laughed and swatted his chest, which was still sheened with sweat from their lovemaking. "Yes, I love you too, silly man. You'd think a billionaire would have more confidence."

"No man has that much confidence when it comes to the one woman who means more than anything. No man feels deserving enough."

"I find that hard to believe," she said, her voice still husky and breathless from calling out his name in the throes of passion.

He chuckled and stroked her hair. "Maybe so. But even a billionaire wants to know he's closed the deal."

"Oh, you closed it. It's final. No going back now," she said, stroking his skin and enjoying the way his breath caught when she did.

"Good," he said, getting a look in his eyes that said he was about ready to close that deal again. "I don't ever want to go back."

She smiled at that and snuggled against him, pressing her breasts into his side, hoping for a little more from him.

But instead, she was disappointed when he stood and got out of bed. She sighed and pushed herself up to sit against the headboard. Her body was still limp from pleasure, and she felt sated and happy.

"Come back here," she said. "Where are you going?"

"Just one last thing to do," he said, rummaging in his bag.

"What?" she asked, unable to fight the curiosity rising in her. "What's going on?" When he didn't answer, she gave him a stern glare. "You know things didn't exactly go that well last time you left me right after lovemaking."

"True," he said. Then he made a little noise of approval and stood with something in his hand. "My parents may not have been mated, but they were married."

"Oh?" Her heart gave a double thump as he walked forward, a small box in his hand. It couldn't be...

He got on his knee. "Will you marry me, Janna?" He took the ring out of the box and held it out. It was an enormous marquis diamond in a platinum mounting with diamonds at the side. "It's my mother's ring, given to me as the oldest child. It would mean everything if you'd wear it until I can claim you for real."

She stared at it for a moment, and he squirmed uncomfortably.

"It's not exactly comfortable on the ground here, Janna," he muttered.

"Oh, I'm sorry! Yes!" She took the ring and threw her arms around him, joining him on the ground. "Of course!" She slid it on her finger, loving the feel of it.

"Thank you," he said, kissing her cheek and smoothing her hair. "Thank you."

"So when do we do this mate claiming thing?" she asked.

"I don't know," he said. "I have to talk to my brothers, see if they know any more than I do about any rules regarding it."

"Well," she said, looking down at the sparkling ring on her finger. "Just let me know. I feel like I could do it tomorrow."

He picked her up and sat down on the bed with her curvaceous body over him. "I'm glad. But I want to make sure it's done right. And when the mate claim is done, then we can get married. Until then, you have my ring and my promise."

"Do you want to be engaged?" she asked. "Do bears need to?"

"Bear *shifter*," he said. "I'm still a man, too. And I want my ring on your finger. I want to keep both bears *and* humans away."

"Aw, come on," she said, teasing him and tickling his chin. "Who would dare mess with Ryder Hart's woman?"

He growled in response. "Hopefully no one."

"After all, it's probably not smart to piss of a bearllionaire," she said, biting her lip to try and not break out into laughter at his look of disgust.

"You didn't…" he said. "You did not just turn me into a pun!" He groaned.

"I did," she said gleefully.

"How long have you been thinking it?" he asked with a long sigh.

"Ever since you asked me to accept the bear and the billionaire. I can't help it. It sort of goes together."

"Except it's impossible to say," he retorted. "Okay, got that out of your system? Good. Never say that abomination again."

"Bearllionaire?" she joked, running a hand down his abs. "Why not? Bearllionaire, bearllionaire, bearllionaire."

She giggled when he growled and flipped her over, pinning her hands over her head. No matter how big he was, he couldn't threaten her. Not now that she knew her grizzly was more of a teddy bear. Unless someone threatened her, that is.

"Say it again. I dare you," he said.

She bit her lip and a smile quirked the corner of her mouth. "Bear—"

He cut her off with a swift kiss and then proceeded to make her forget anything about the word bearllionaire.

Except it was an excellent way to rile him up in a most delicious way.

And luckily, it seemed she'd have forever to do that.

EPILOGUE

Three Months Later

IT WAS A SNOWY, FROZEN day in spring when Janna and Ryder completed the mate claiming.

Janna's friends were finally accepting that she really was doubling down on this whirlwind romance and marrying Ryder. And her family, though doubtful, didn't affect Janna's excitement for the future.

She wore white, like a wedding dress, because she'd wanted to look beautiful for Ryder on this most special day. The last few months had just justified her in her decision to be with him. Each day was more wonderful. That didn't mean there were never disagreements, but that was okay between two people who were committed to staying together and who knew the overall relationship was more important than any one issue.

More than anything, Janna knew she was happier than she'd ever been before. Ryder had said the same, on occasion. Though he still tended to be stuffy and shy when overwhelmed with emotion. It worked for him in business and was a hard habit to break.

But every once in while, he could be mushy, vulnerable, in a way that melted her heart.

She wore a white faux fur coat that was thick and kept her wool dress warm. And thick white boots lined with lamb's wool. When Ryder approached, in his bear form, huge and magnificent but with that familiar look in his eyes that made her heart melt, she sighed and walked forward.

"This is so stupid," Riley said, putting a hand to his forehead. "How can anyone know they'll be able to do this forever?"

Ryan quietly stuck out an arm and shoved Riley off the top of the mountain while they were waiting.

Riley's shout turned into a snarl, and a few moments later, he came huffing over the ridge in bear form. "What'd you do that for, asshole?"

"You're ruining their special moment," Ryan said. "And the scenery."

"Mph," Riley said. "I mean, I get Janna is awesome. One of a kind. But I'm never going to understand wanting just one woman when you can have dozens."

Ryan shook his head in disgust, but Ryder threw back his head and laughed.

"You'll know it when it happens to you," he said, taking another step closer to his mate so she could complete the ceremony. He loved that she looked at him with love. That she wasn't afraid of his bear. Wasn't intimidated by his success nor affected by it.

She truly accepted him for him, just as he'd accepted and wanted her from the moment he met her. And in a few moments, it'd be complete for forever.

"That'll never happen to me," Riley retorted.

If his brother would just shut up. "Does Ryan need to push you down the ledge again?" Ryder growled.

Riley snapped his mouth shut. "No."

So watched by his brothers, one in bear form, one in human, they completed the ritual. Janna walked forward to his bear, whispered words as she caressed his face, and placed a kiss at the side of his face. His cheek.

In doing this, she was accepting his bear. Warmth soared through him even as a cold mountain breeze swept over the scene. After this, they would mate, as humans, somewhere private, and they'd be sealed together for life.

But more than anything, Ryder felt more accepted than he'd ever felt in his life, and as Janna pulled back and looked at him with sparkling eyes, he knew he'd found a happiness that he'd protect forever.

"I love you," he said, transforming to his human form as his brother placed a blanket around him.

"I love you, too," she said.

"Forever."

"Forever."

Riley coughed, and Ryan cleared his throat, and Ryder sent them both a glare that said they should get lost.

Five minutes later, two large grizzlies could be seen running helter skelter down the mountain.

"They'll get it someday," Ryder said, watching them in the distance, holding Janna close.

"Maybe." She looked up at him. "Ryder?"

"Yes?" he said, eyeing his mate.

"Take me home."

"Yes, ma'am." So he did, carrying her to the cabin nearby. It wasn't home in the traditional sense of the word because they wouldn't be living there.

But it was home because it was a place where they could come together in a special way. Safe from the world and protected.

A little later, Ryder held Janna in his arms, warm and content to have the most important woman in the world to him finally his at last, forever.

She snuggled into his chest and said she loved him and then fell asleep.

Ryder let out a sigh of satisfaction. Janna was now his home. He could only hope his brothers found the same one day.

The bearllionaire smiled happily, curled around his mate, and fell asleep.

Made in the USA
San Bernardino, CA
06 March 2020